"Kissing

Josh admitted. "   ou, being with Meg

Right for *now*, Libby was sure, though she didn't say it. She didn't want to argue with Josh. As a matter of fact, she didn't really want to talk at all. Because talking made her worry about how much it would hurt after Christmas, when Josh was gone.

No, she didn't want to talk, didn't want to think. She just wanted to kiss him.

When she was kissing Josh, she could forget the inner voice that kept whispering that she and her daughter would be heartbroken when he left. While she was in his arms, she could think of nothing but him.

And, for the moment, that had to be enough....

Dear Reader,

Although it will be archived by now, I've been writing to readers on our www.eHarlequin.com community bulletin boards about Silhouette Romance and what makes it so special. Readers like the emotion, the strength of the heroines, the truly heroic nature of the men and a quick, yet satisfying, read. I'm delighted that Silhouette Romance is able to fulfill a few of your fantasies! Be sure to stop by our site. :)

I hope you had a chance to revisit *Lion on the Prowl* by Kasey Michaels when it was out last month in a special collection with Heather Graham's *Lucia in Love*. Be sure not to miss a glimpse into those characters' lives with this month's lively spin-off called *Bachelor on the Prowl*. Elizabeth Harbison gives us *A Pregnant Proposal* from our continuity HAVING THE BOSS'S BABY. Look out next month for *The Makeover Takeover* by Sandra Paul.

Other stories this month include the second title in Lilian Darcy's THE CINDERELLA CONSPIRACY. Be assured that *Saving Cinderella* has the heartwarming emotion and strong heroes that Lilian Darcy delivers every time! And Carol Grace has spun off a title from *Fit for a Sheik*. This month, look for *Taming the Sheik*.

And we've got a Christmas treat to get you in the mood for the holidays. Carolyn Greene has *Her Mistletoe Man* while new-to-the-line author Holly Jacobs asks *Do You Hear What I Hear?*

I hope that you enjoy these stories, and keep in touch.

Mary-Theresa Hussey

Mary-Theresa Hussey,
Senior Editor

Please address questions and book requests to:
Silhouette Reader Service
U.S.: 3010 Walden Ave., P.O. Box 1325, Buffalo, NY 14269
Canadian: P.O. Box 609, Fort Erie, Ont. L2A 5X3

Do You Hear What I Hear?

HOLLY JACOBS

SILHOUETTE *Romance*®

Published by Silhouette Books

America's Publisher of Contemporary Romance

For Miss Mac, Joan McLaughlin, who saw more in me
than I saw in myself. You are sorely missed.

And for Allison Lyons
whose input and insight so enriched this story.

 SILHOUETTE BOOKS

ISBN 0-373-19557-5

DO YOU HEAR WHAT I HEAR?

Copyright © 2001 by Holly Fuhrman

This edition published by arrangement with Harlequin Books S.A.

Visit Silhouette at www.eHarlequin.com

Printed in U.S.A.

HOLLY JACOBS

can't remember a time when she didn't read...and read a lot. Writing her own stories just seemed a natural outgrowth of that love. Reading, writing and chauffeuring kids to and from activities makes for a busy life. But it's one she wouldn't trade for any other.

Holly lives in Erie, Pennsylvania, with her husband, four children and a two-hundred-pound Old English mastiff. In her "spare" time, Holly loves hearing from her fans. You can write to her at P.O. Box 11102, Erie, PA 16514-1102.

Dear Reader,

This is my first Silhouette Romance novel, and I'm so pleased to be a part of this great line. Writing stories about love and family is a perfect niche for me. I married my high school sweetheart and we have four wonderful children ranging from college age to grade school. Add to that a two-hundred-pound mastiff, and you may guess that there's never a dull moment at our house!

Reading has always been a part of my life. When I was in the third grade I read a biography of Helen Keller and knew I'd found a role model. She was a woman who faced hurdles in her life, but she didn't let them trip her up. No, she overcame them all and triumphed. I can't tell you how much she inspired me. Incorporating a hearing-impaired character in my first Silhouette Romance novel is a small tribute to her, and to every family who has ever overcome tremendous obstacles.

I hope you enjoy *Do You Hear What I Hear?* and that you'll look for my upcoming Silhouette and Harlequin titles.

Wally Jacobs

Chapter One

"Have you met him?"

"Him who?" Libby McGuiness asked as she measured a section of Mabel's gray hair on the right side against its counterpart on the left side.

"Your new neighbor," Mabel said, her exasperation evident in her tone.

"No, I haven't met him yet, though I met his receptionist and she seemed nice enough."

"Well, *nice* isn't the word I'd use to describe Dr. Gardner. Hunk—now that's a good description."

Libby chuckled. Mabel might be a widow pushing seventy, but she had the vitality of someone in her twenties. An acupuncturist who vowed never to retire, Mabel was a vital part of the downtown Erie small business community; more than that, she was a friend—a friend whose main goal in life was finding Libby a man.

"You could use a hunk," Mabel added.

"A hunk of money, that's for sure." Owning her own salon, Snips and Snaps, might be satisfying, but it wasn't always overly lucrative.

Libby turned the chair a full one hundred and eighty degrees. Satisfied that everything was even and in place, she turned Mabel to the mirror. "What do you think?"

"It's perfect," the older woman said, fluffing her new cut. "But then, it always is when you cut my hair. Maybe you should take a look at your new neighbor. He might be perfect, as well."

"I'm glad you think your hair is perfect, and thanks for the suggestion about the doctor, but I'll pass. There may be such a thing as a perfect haircut, but there's no such thing as a perfect man."

Libby whipped off the cape that covered Mabel, and led her to the register. "Do you want to make your next appointment now?"

"You're sure about the doctor? I could introduce you."

Libby chuckled. "I'm absolutely positive."

Mabel sighed. "Do you have any openings for a wash and style before Thanksgiving?"

Libby checked her appointment book. "I can squeeze you in Wednesday at four-thirty. You'll be it for the week."

"You're a dear. All the kids are coming home for the holiday, and Stacy is bringing her new boyfriend, so I want to look my best." She handed Libby a twenty. "And speaking of best, maybe you should do something new with your hair before you meet Dr. Hunk."

"I'm sure I'll meet our new neighbor, but I don't plan on *meeting* him, if you know what I mean. And I know you know what I mean. I like my hair just the way it is," she said, fingering her long braid. "And I like my life just the way it is, as well. But thanks for the advice."

Libby pulled Mabel's change out of the drawer, but the older woman just waved it away. "You keep it, dear. You did a lovely job."

Mabel's matchmaking might be blatant, but it was hard to stay annoyed with such a generous, sweet spirit. "Thanks, Mabel. I'll see you for that wash and style."

"See you then. And think about what I said."

Libby tucked the bills into her pocket. The only thinking she planned on thinking about was Meg's new computer. She'd been saving tips since the beginning of the year for this one special Christmas present. Not just any computer, but something big and fast—something that would put the world at her daughter's fingertips.

Meg. Yes, that's all she was going to think about. Meg and Libby were a team, and they didn't need any man messing up their lives. So Mabel could just keep her hunk.

Libby glanced at her watch. Just another hour until she was home and with Meg. As much as she loved Snips and Snaps, she loved going home to her daughter even more.

Home? Just how was she supposed to get there, Libby thought an hour later as she eyed the green truck with Ohio plates that was butted up against the bumper of her Neon.

How was she supposed to get out of the parallel parking space with no room to maneuver? The idiot who had parked that truck was clearly encroaching on her parking space. It wasn't her fault that he drove a truck the size of a small tank and had to take up more than his fair share of the parking space.

And look at that—he had about two feet of free space behind him. Couldn't he at least have given some of it to her?

Libby realized she was mentally referring to her bumper-pusher as a male. Maybe it was sexist, but she'd bet a week's pay it was a guy. A big-truck-driving, thinks-he's-macho, parking-space-hogging man.

Libby glanced nervously at her watch. She was going to be late picking Meg up from the Hendersons. Where was a cop when she needed one? The police station was just across the square. There should be one of Erie's finest somewhere about. This green-truck jerk deserved a ticket.

Better yet, forget the cop. Where was a tow truck?

No one was going to ride to her rescue. She'd just have to call the Hendersons and explain she was trapped until the driver of the red Jeep in front of her, or the idiot green-truck's driver came out. She hoped it was the truck's driver. She really wanted to give him a piece of her mind, not that she had much to spare, Meg would have added.

Thinking of her daughter's occasional wisecracks made Libby smile, despite her annoyance. Then a cold gust of wind made her remember why she was annoyed in the first place.

Well, she might have to wait, but she wasn't waiting outside. November's Canadian wind blew off Lake Erie and made things far too cold to do much more than hurry from one warm place to another. She crawled into her Neon and started it, cranking the heat up to the highest setting. She might as well be comfortable while she waited. Hopefully this wouldn't take too long. At five o'clock the city pretty much shut down, so one of the cars would probably be leaving soon.

Just as she reached for her cell phone, she spotted a man coming out of Gardner's Ophthalmology and headed for the green truck. She jumped from her car. "Hey, you."

The man looked up. He was gorgeous. Drop-dead-drag-your-tongue-on-the-street gorgeous.

"Yes?" he asked with a smile—a smile that made him even better looking, though it shouldn't be possible.

Good-looking or not, Libby's anger didn't fade.

"I don't know how you park in Ohio, but here in Pennsylvania we at least give the other person a foot or so to maneuver."

"Really?" he asked blandly.

"Really."

"I'll keep that in mind." He opened the truck door and started to climb in.

"That's all? No *I'm sorry.* No *I won't let it happen again*?"

He sighed and stood beside his open door. "Listen, I've had a very long day and don't need to have some shrew—"

"Shrew?"

"—yapping at me because she doesn't know how to parallel park."

"My car was here first. You're the one crawling up my bumper, and yet you have the nerve to say I don't know how to park?"

"Well, I don't know how you do it here in Pennsylvania, but in Ohio we try to come within a foot of the curb."

"I'm within a foot of the curb. Heck, I'm practically on the curb. And how close I am to the curb doesn't affect how others park and, more importantly, get out of their parking spaces.''

He climbed into the truck. "So maybe next time you should park on the parking ramp at the corner of Eighth and Peach. It's only a couple of blocks.''

Libby knocked on the window, and reluctantly the parking idiot rolled the glass down. "Or, maybe,'' she said, "next time you should park there when you visit the doctor's.''

"That's a heck of a hike to walk to the office every day.''

"You need to see the ophthalmologist every day?'' Right. The man didn't have glasses; she'd wager not even contacts. No, Mr. Perfect's eyes were probably twenty-twenty. Who did he think he was fooling?''

"I *am* the ophthalmologist.''

"Dr. Gardner?'' This was Mabel's Dr. Hunk? Well, he might be eye candy, but he certainly left a bitter aftertaste.

He nodded. "And you are?''

"Your new neighbor, Libby McGuiness.''

"You have an apartment here?'' He nodded toward the apartments that topped a number of the square's businesses.

"No, I own Snips and Snaps, the beauty salon right next door to you. And since it appears we'll both be parking here frequently, maybe you should invest in some parking lessons.''

"Only if you join me,'' he said pleasantly.

Libby resisted the urge to stick her tongue out at the man and attempted to sound mature. "Listen, sparring with you hasn't been much of an exercise in wits, since you've only got half of yours, but I have to go. If you wouldn't mind moving your truck…?"

"And I have to confess, this is the nicest welcome to the neighborhood I've had to date."

A small shot of guilt coursed through her. After all, she might not want to go after Dr. Gardner in a romantic way, but she also didn't want to alienate a neighbor.

Libby's guilt totally evaporated when the parking-failure doctor shot her a snotty grin.

"With manners like yours, I'm sure you're in store for even better ones," Libby said before she stormed to her car.

Mabel wanted her to change her hair for hunky Dr. Gardner? Libby slammed the car door shut. The only thing she'd change was her parking space. She had a daughter to pick up and couldn't wait on a daily basis for Dr. Gardner to move his truck.

The green truck slipped smoothly into Reverse then, and with the two feet of free space behind it, angled out of the parking space. Finally able to back up, Libby followed suit. It was time to go home.

A half hour later she stood in her kitchen with Meg, and the parking-idiot was all but forgotten.

"And then Jenny barfed, right there in the class. The janitor had to come clean it up. We had class in the cafeteria then because the room still smelled, but the cafeteria smelled almost as bad.''

Some things never changed. Bad cafeteria food was one of those things.

Libby glanced at her daughter's brunette curls. Another thing that never changed, and never would, was the delight she got watching Meg. Every year she just seemed more wonderful. Her baby was ten years old. Where had the time gone?

"Do you have homework?" Libby asked to cover up the fact she was suddenly feeling nostalgic. Ten-year-olds didn't appreciate being sighed over.

Meg frowned. "You ask me that every night. Maybe I did it at the Hendersons?"

Libby stirred the sauce and smiled. Her daughter was a normal ten-year-old girl in every sense of the word. She put the spoon down and said, "And maybe you didn't. Which is it?"

"Fine. I'll do my homework." Meg's hands moved much slower than when they recited Jenny's barf experience.

"Dinner's on in about fifteen minutes, so get to it," Libby said as she signed.

Moving fingers. Dancing hands. Those signs were the only indication that there was something different about Meg.

She watched her daughter stomp away and couldn't help but smile again. Meg groused about homework, had a room that resembled a pigsty and spent as much time as she could manage chatting with her friends on the Internet. Libby wouldn't allow her to use public chat rooms, but they'd set up a private one where all Meg's friends could meet. And meet they did whenever Meg could sneak some computer time on their antiquated model.

She'd be thrilled with the new model Libby planned to buy her for Christmas. Computers, sign language, lip reading—Libby encouraged anything that opened communication for her daughter.

She started slicing the Italian bread, visions of modems and mouses floating through her head. Like any other fifth grader, Meg would love a faster model.

Like any other fifth grader. That phrase summed up Meggie to a T. Well, maybe not just like any other fifth grader. Meg was special, and it wasn't her hearing impairment that made her that way. She was just a very special little girl.

Too bad her father, Mitch, hadn't stuck around long enough to see that he was right—their daughter wasn't normal. No, Meg was spectacular.

Mitch's loss was Libby's gain. Raising Meg was probably the most wonderful thing she'd ever do. Getting dinner with her, nagging her about homework, seeing the world through her daughter's baby blue eyes was a gift. And Libby tried not to let a day go by without reminding herself how blessed she was.

Fifteen minutes later the two of them sat down to their spaghetti and meatballs. In between bites Meg bubbled about her score on some new computer game she was playing with Jackie Henderson: "I beat her, big-time."

"I suppose she'll want a rematch, and she might win, so don't get too cocky."

"No way. My fingers are quicker than hers will ever be."

After nine years of signing, Libby's fingers were fast, but not nearly as fast as Meg's. She was probably right—Jackie didn't stand a chance.

The kitchen light flashed at the same moment the doorbell buzzer sounded.

"I'll get it," Meg signed even as she flew out of her chair before Libby could protest. She didn't like Meg answering the door after dark, and evenings came early in November. She hastily trailed after her daughter.

"Flowers!" Meg signed before she took the arrangement of fall foliage from the deliveryman.

The dark-haired deliveryman flashed a lopsided smile as he checked his clipboard. "Libby McGuiness, right?"

"Right." Libby fished in her back pocket and pulled out a couple dollars. "Here," she said, thrusting the bills at him. "Thank you."

"You're welcome, ma'am. Whoever he is, he's sure sorry. He called the shop and sent me out after hours, even though it cost him extra."

Libby shut the door and took the card from the arrangement Meg had placed on the hall table. "Dear Ms. Snippy," it read, "Here's a number for Dan's Driving Lessons. I suggest you start ASAP."

What an arrogant, couldn't-park-to-save-his-truck sort of man. Without thinking she bent and sniffed the flowers. He might be an idiot, but that didn't mean Libby couldn't enjoy the beautiful arrangement.

"What?" Meg asked, grabbing the card.

"I had a run-in at work," Libby explained, all her previous annoyance flooding back. "Come on, let's finish dinner." She stuffed the card in her pocket and started walking back to the kitchen.

Meg stopped her with a tug on her sleeve. "An accident?" Concern was etched on Meg's expressive face.

"No," Libby reassured her. "A very bad parker who thinks he's funny."

"I think he is, too," Meg said. "Is he cute?"

"No, he's not cute, and you're a traitor."

"I've seen you park." Meg pantomimed numerous parking attempts. "You end up miles from the curb."

"And you're grounded," Libby said, laughing. Her frustration with Dr. Hunky-can't-park Gardner evaporated in the face of her daughter's amusement.

"Am not."

"Are, too." Hands flew as they talked over one another. "No." "Yes." "I still have homework." "You're a cheat." "And you can't park."

"Eat," Libby said, and Meg's hands quieted as she

finished her spaghetti. Unfortunately Libby's thoughts didn't have to quiet while she ate, and no matter how she tried, they kept circling back to Dr. Gardner. He obviously thought his good looks and a cute card attached to some mums and leaves would get him out of trouble. Well, he had a thing or two left to learn.

Libby didn't like him—didn't like him a bit. He was arrogant, and he had a warped sense of humor. Add to that the fact he was far too good-looking for his own good, probably had half of Erie's female population eating out of his hand, and you had the right mixture for trouble.

Okay, he just moved here. So, he might not have all that many women yet, but just give him time and he would. But one of those women would never be Libby McGuiness.

She could sense trouble when she met it, and in this case trouble had a name—Dr. Gardner.

Trouble.

The pattern of the waiting room border was the least of his worries the next morning, but Joshua Gardner found himself staring at the wallpaper book anyway. Visions of wallpaper designs might be dancing before his eyes, but it was visions of his new neighbor that kept dancing in his mind. A new neighbor whose snapping blue eyes had haunted his dreams last night. A new neighbor who didn't appreciate his parking abilities.

She did have a point. It certainly hadn't been his best parking job ever. He'd been in such a hurry to get into his office—*his office*—that he'd simply jostled his truck into the first available space and never even checked that the oversize vehicle hadn't infringed on anyone else's space.

And, of course, his response to her anger had been a bit over the top. He'd been tired, and the tension of getting his practice off the ground might not impress her as a good enough excuse, but there it was. He'd been tired and grumpy and she'd simply set his teeth on edge.

Josh had felt bad moments after he'd pulled out of his parking space. He hoped his flowers had eased the tension between them. The last thing he wanted was to start off on the wrong foot—or tires as the case may be—with his new neighbors.

She was cute though. *Ms. McGuiness.* She was all bristles and outrage. Both of which happened to look very good on her. He chuckled as he forced his attention back to the task at hand. Wallpaper. It might not be one of his most earth-shattering decisions, but it was his decision. His new life, his new office...his new wallpaper border.

"This," he said, pointing to a bold, geometric-shaped border.

"You're sure?" Amy's tone suggested she was anything but sure about his choice.

"Yes. I'm positive."

His cute, just-out-of-high-school, bundle-of-energy receptionist shrugged and grabbed the book. "Okay, you're the boss. It's your office." She strode from the office and slammed the door.

The boss.

That was him. Joshua Gardner was in charge, in control. It had been a long time since he'd felt as if he was in control of anything. But now he was the sole owner of Gardner's Ophthalmology. Every piece of furniture and all the equipment in the office was his. The hiring and firing of staff for the office was all up to him. Even the wallpaper decisions were all his. The buck stopped at his desk.

The problem was the bucks were close to stopping altogether. Buying Dr. Master's practice, deciding to buy the office building rather than rent it, relocating to Erie… It all took money. After his divorce, his bank account was suddenly lighter than it had been in years. At the moment it wasn't just light, it was next to empty. But the practice came with a built-in patient base, so hopefully he'd recoup some of his money soon.

Joshua glanced around his office, most of his things still in boxes. The painters were coming tonight to give the waiting room and his office a badly needed face-lift. His new border—which was perfect no matter what Amy thought—would go up sometime next week. Things were progressing.

The move had been the right thing to do. Coming

home to Erie, Pennsylvania, had been just what he'd needed to begin his life anew in the city where he'd begun his life. If he walked to the corner and looked down the road, he could see the hospital he was born in. Farther down State Street was the bay where he'd learned to water-ski. Happy memories were stored in about every corner of the city.

Dr. Joshua Gardner was home, he was in charge of his destiny and things were going to be great.

The intercom buzzed. "Doctor?"

"Yes, Amy."

"Your eight o'clock is here."

"I'm coming." Josh shoved his papers to the back of the desk. He was home, doing the job he loved to do, and had probably even scored a few brownie points with his new neighbor with his flowers. Every woman loved to get flowers.

Yes, things were going to be just great.

Chapter Two

"So, what do you think?"

Eight o'clock in the morning was too early to think, too early to deal with Mabel, too early to deal with just about anything. That's why Libby never scheduled her first hair appointment until eight-thirty if she could help it. Coffee and paperwork for half an hour. It was quiet and eased her into a fully functional human.

And if customers were too much to deal with, Mabel was a complete overload of her fragile system.

Libby finished scooping the coffee into the filter, trying to come up with a convincing reason why she couldn't help Mabel out. "I don't think—"

It's a good idea. That's how Libby had planned to end the sentence, but Mabel cut her off and said, "So don't think. Just say yes. It will be fun."

"If it's going to be so much fun, why don't you do it?" Libby slammed the filter into the coffeemaker and hit the switch.

"Hey, I'm president of the association, I can't hog all the fun jobs. And I'm doing my bit for the area. Now it's your turn."

"Couldn't I find some other turn to take? I could plan a bake sale, or—"

"You could plan the Christmas party." Mabel shook a motherly finger at Libby. "I need someone I know I can count on."

"But I don't have the time." Time. Libby felt as if every day was a race against the clock. All day long on her feet, then her evenings with Meg, and all the responsibility for the household chores and...

Libby shook her head. No, she didn't have time for anything else.

"What if I got someone to co-chair the event?" Mabel asked.

Mabel wasn't going to give up. Libby could see it in the older woman's stubborn expression and realized she'd lost this particular battle before she'd even started fighting.

Facing the inevitable, she asked, "Someone who'll co-chair in name only, or someone who is willing to dig in and really work?"

"Work." Mabel held up her fingers in a scout's honor sign and then crossed her heart.

If the woman had a heart she would never have

come to Libby and made this absurd request in the first place. Despite the fact that everything in her was screaming to refuse, Libby found herself saying, "Maybe, if I'm not doing everything all by myself, I could manage."

"Of course you can," Mabel promised. "This is a good way for you to have some fun. We all worry about you. All you do is work and take care of Meg. You need a life."

"And planning a Christmas party is your way of assuring I get a life?"

Mabel shrugged even as she broke into a grin. "It's a start. And if you have any problems or questions, you know you just have to ask."

The coffeemaker made the *glug, glug* sound that indicated it was done brewing. Gratefully Libby poured herself a mug. If Mabel had come after her first few cups, she suspected she would have done a better job of getting out of this particular task.

"If I have questions, you'll have the answer?" she asked.

"Of course not. I'm a delegator, not a problem solver." Mabel grinned infectiously. "But I'll sympathize."

"Gee, you're too generous."

Mabel shrugged. "It's a fault."

"Do you want a cup?" Libby asked, but Mabel shook her head. "You know it's going to be your fault if this party is a bust. I don't throw personal parties, so what do I know about throwing one for around fifty people?"

"As much as anyone else, I'm afraid. And, Libby?"

Something in Mabel's tone made Libby even more concerned. She took a fortifying gulp of coffee. "Yes?"

"Um, I did mention that this Christmas party isn't just for the group?"

"No?" It was for more than the dozen or so businesses, and their employees, that made up the Perry Square Small Business Association?

"Families, too."

"Mabel!" Quickly Libby's mind tried to come up with some calculations. The Perry Square Business Association, the PSBA, had a dozenish businesses as members, about fifty people. If families were included, that was definitely over a hundred people.

"Just how many people am I planning for?" Libby asked.

"Oh, I don't know. Somewhere under two hundred. And don't worry. I'll have a list of kids for you, and their ages."

Libby glared at the woman she used to consider a friend. "Why do I need the children's ages?"

"So Santa can have the appropriate presents there for them."

"Presents?" What on earth had she gotten herself into? "Mabel, you didn't say anything about families, or kids or presents. I was thinking a brunch at some restaurant, maybe a party favor or two. There's no way—''

''—you could do it alone, which is why the idea of a co-chair is such a good one.'' Mabel must have sensed she'd best get while the getting was good, because she grabbed her coat and started toward the door.

''Oh, no you don't,'' Libby called. ''We're not done talking here.''

''Now, don't you worry. I've got a couple great lists that should prove very helpful. And it just so happens that I suddenly have the perfect idea for a co-chair for you.''

''Who?'' Libby tried to think of anyone in their group who was crazy enough to let Mabel rope them in. She couldn't think of a soul…other than herself.

''I don't want to say until I'm sure.'' Mabel's hand was on the doorknob.

''Mabel, you're making me nervous.''

Mabel turned around and faced Libby with a look of confusion on her face. ''You know, people say I make them nervous all the time and I'm not sure why.''

''Maybe it has to do with your coming at them with needles, or maybe you just have one of those personalities that makes people nervous.'' Realizing that Mabel had managed to get her off the subject of the Christmas party, Libby added, ''About this party—''

"Gotta go," said the neighborhood needle-pushing acupuncturist and busybody as she raced out the door.

Libby watched helplessly as Mabel disappeared from the front of the store. Plan a Christmas party? What had she been thinking?

She'd have to worry about it later, because she had a full day's schedule waiting for her. But worry about it she would.

There was just no way she could plan a party for two hundred in just a few weeks. The shop would be a madhouse between Thanksgiving and Christmas. Most of the time Libby looked forward to the holidays. But suddenly she was feeling decidedly Grinchy about this Christmas party.

Grinchy wasn't the word to describe how Libby felt as she waited for her four-thirty appointment later that day.

"What do you want now?" she barked when parking-space-hogging Dr. Gardner waltzed into the shop and took a seat in front of her.

"Just a quick trim."

Realization hit her. "I saw J. Gardner in the appointment book, but I didn't realize it was you." The name had been in Josie's handwriting. Libby should have asked who the customer was when she didn't recognize the name.

If Pearly and Josie weren't in the back room, she'd

be giving them the evil eye, hoping to make them worry about a lecture when this new *customer* left.

"Believe it or not, Doctor isn't my first name. Most of my friends call me Joshua, or Josh even."

"Then I think I'll stick to Dr. Gardner, if you don't mind."

He was watching her reflection in the mirror, Libby realized. His dark brown eyes studied her, making her feel like a hare being stalked by a hawk.

"And if I said I did mind, Libby?" he asked softly.

"Then I'd say, so sorry, Dr. Gardner, I prefer we keep things formal." She whipped the cape around his neck, and pulled it closed with a little more force than required. "And the name's Ms. McGuiness."

He sighed. "You're still miffed about the parking space."

"Miffed?" She reached for a comb, tapping the excess sterilizer solution against the side of the soaking jar.

"The flowers as an apology didn't help? In my experience, women love that kind of thing. Plus, I had to go to the effort of looking up your address in the phone book."

"I realize that alphabetical order might cause you some difficulty, so I'll give you credit for having to figure out just where McGuiness might be in the phone book. And I might admit I love flowers, though I hate to be a generalization, but your card just added insult to injury."

From anyone else she might have found the card humorous, even cute, but from Dr. My-smile-gets-me-out-of-trouble Gardner, she was simply even more put out.

Libby stared at his hair a moment, strangely reluctant to touch him. Why was that? Of course he was good-looking, but she cut a lot of good-looking men's hair and never felt this unreasonable need to keep as much distance as possible between herself and them. Men didn't affect her—not anymore. She was totally immune to the whole species.

"An apology added insult to injury?" He craned his head so he could look her in the eye. "How?"

"Dr. Gardner, if I'd seen an apology, I'd have accepted it." Forcing herself to shake the crazy urge to run as far away as she could get, Libby reached out and turned Dr. Gardner's head so he was facing forward. "The card was just another slap in the face."

"You don't have much of a sense of humor, do you, *Ms. McGuiness?*"

"Sure I do, when I see something humorous."

The only funny thing she saw right now was the strange emotions Dr. Gardner seemed to be evoking in her. She wasn't the type to start fights on the street, and she wasn't the type to hold a grudge, and yet holding one she was—holding on to it as tightly as she possibly could.

"Are you saying I'm not funny?" he asked.

"I'm saying you're certainly funny, just not in a humorous sense of the word."

"I'll have you know that plenty of women find me humorous."

Libby realized that Josie and Pearly were probably in the back room hanging on every word of her conversation with the irritating Dr. Gardner. Determined not to give them anything else worth listening to, she finished the absurd argument. "I'm sure they do, Dr. Gardner. I'm sure they do. But the big laughs you give other women don't interest me at all. What kind of cut you want does."

"Like I said before, just a trim." The humor in his voice had faded, replaced by a clipped annoyance.

"You're sure you're comfortable trusting me with a sharp implement at your neck?" Libby was sure she wouldn't trust the good doctor. His frustration was evident by his expression.

"I'm sure you're much too professional to maim a paying customer."

"Fine." Finally the man shut up. Libby spritzed his hair with her water bottle, then snipped in blessed silence.

Joshua Gardner might not be as humorous as he liked to think, but Libby would admit the man had a fine head of hair. Thick, with a slight tendency to curl. Running her fingers through it would be a pure sensual delight if she was the kind of woman who paid attention to those kind of things. But Libby didn't pay attention to the way the ends of his hair curled around her fingers. No, not one bit of attention.

No wonder he kept his hair well trimmed. Otherwise it would rapidly get out of control, just as her strange thoughts were out of control.

She toyed with the hair, just making sure she'd cut it evenly, she assured herself. That was the only reason her fingers were lingering in his hair. It had nothing to do with the pleasure of running her fingers through his dark locks. Not a thing.

"Are you done fondling me?" Joshua finally asked, pulling Libby from her hair-induced daze.

"If you didn't want me to touch you, why on earth did you make an appointment to have me cut your hair?" She spun the chair so it faced her rather than the mirror.

"I made the appointment because I thought I could kill two birds with one stone. Get a much-needed trim and discuss what we're going to do about the party."

"What party?"

Joshua stuck out his hand. "Hi. Joshua Gardner, co-chairman of the PSBA Christmas party."

Libby ignored the hand. "I'll kill her."

"I could ask her who, but I'm going to assume you mean Mabel. And I'm going to assume the fact you want to kill her indicates you're less than enthused at the prospect of working with me. Since planning a Christmas party requires very little parallel parking, I think we should be safe." He shot her a smile, one that had probably gotten him out of countless sticky situations.

Despite the fact that a smiling, newly trimmed Joshua Gardner was a sight to behold, Libby frowned. "I quit."

His smile slipped a notch. "What?"

"You can plan the party yourself."

There. Problem solved. Libby hadn't wanted to plan the Christmas party before she found out who her co-chair would be, but now...well, having a mammogram was higher on her list of things she wanted to do. At least a mammogram had some intrinsic value, something she'd found totally lacking in Joshua Gardner. Unless she considered his great head of hair—which Libby definitely wasn't considering.

"I don't know the area," Joshua protested. "I mean, I might be from Erie, but things have changed since I left home."

"I'm sure you can find someone else to help you."

Josie and Pearly had been quiet in the back room—too quiet. She was betting either of them would willingly throw themselves at the man's feet, and help plan the party.

"I'm sure one of my employees would volunteer."

A small thud came from the back—a thud she was sure her two employees were responsible for. Whether it was Pearly and Josie thumping, *Sure we'll do it* or *What are you thinking?* Libby wasn't sure. The only thing she was sure of was that she didn't want to spend any more time than necessary with Dr. Gardner.

"What are you afraid of, Libby?" he asked quietly.

"Ms. McGuiness," she corrected. "And I'm not afraid of anything. You just rub me the wrong way, and I don't have the time or patience to pretend your arrogant, overbearing manner is acceptable. So, keep your flowers, your hair and your smiles to yourself. And find someone else to help with the party."

"Are you telling me that you are immature enough to let one small incident mar any further relationship between us?"

He removed the cape and stood, facing Libby. She had to crane her neck to look him in the eyes, but look him in the eyes she did. "Let me assure you, Dr. Gardner, I have no interest in a relationship with you. You might think that no woman can resist you, but I'm quite capable. I have no desire—"

"I wasn't talking about a personal relationship," he interrupted. "I was talking about a professional relationship. We're both members of the Perry Square Business Association, and we're neighbors. Surely you're adult enough to put one small disagreement behind us, and work together on this one little party. Unless you're avoiding me for some other reason."

Libby knew a challenge when she heard one. She shouldn't care what he thought, as long as he thought it somewhere she wasn't. But despite the fact she should just let him think whatever his tiny little mind wanted to think, she found herself saying, "Fine."

"Fine. You'll stay my co-chairman?"

"Yes. But no more flowers, no more parking anywhere near my car and we keep our meetings as brief as possible and strictly business."

Again, Joshua extended his hand and this time, reluctantly, Libby accepted it in an impersonal handshake.

"Partners," he simply said.

"For now," she added.

"Thanks for the haircut." He reached in his pocket and handed her a bill. "Will that cover it?"

"Just let me get you your change."

"Keep it. Could we meet tomorrow night after work?"

Libby wanted to say no to both the tip and the meeting. But the tip would go toward Meg's computer, and tomorrow was Friday and Meg was spending the night with the Hendersons, so it was convenient. But it irked her to tell the good doctor so.

"Fine," she said grudgingly.

"Fine. I'll see you tomorrow after work, *Ms. McGuiness.*" He turned and left the store.

As if every ounce of energy had drained away, Libby sank into the chair that was still warm with Joshua Gardner's body heat.

"Way to go, honey," Pearly said as she burst from the back room.

"For a minute there, I thought you'd blown it." Josie patted her hair. Her opinion was, bigger was better, and her red-from-a-bottle hair was certainly proof of that philosophy. Despite its impressive height, there was never a strand out of place. Josie's nails were as loud as her hair, and just about as big and red. As the shop's manicurist, she felt her nails were advertisement, and she advertised as much as she could. "I mean, Mabel found the perfect guy for you to work with."

"Perfect?" Libby snorted. "He's overbearing, arrogant, very unhumorous in his I-think-I'm-soooo-funny way, and—"

"Flowers. Tell us about the flowers," Pearly commanded. Pearly, the shop's other hairstylist, still carried her Georgia roots in every word she uttered, just as she carried her own natural graying brunette hair. Pearly didn't believe in pretenses, not even with hair color. Soft and very Southern, Pearly was a lady to the core of her being.

"You two were eavesdropping." The accusation held very little heat. Libby was well aware that Pearly and Josie were professional eavesdroppers and busybodies. That's why they got along with Mabel so well. There was no way they would have been able to resist the opportunity to spy.

"Of course we were spying," Josie said, honest to the core.

"You should have just gone home. You didn't have any more appointments," she grumbled.

"And miss all the action?" Josie laughed. "I don't think so."

"What was that thump back there?"

"Me kicking the wall," Josie admitted. "I thought you'd blown it."

"I wish I had." Libby rubbed her temple. Dealing with Joshua Gardner had given her a headache. Dealing with Josie and Pearly was intensifying it.

"Honey, when fate throws a good-looking man in your lap, it's best to catch him." Pearly was always spouting off down-home wisdom.

"Personally I've found it best to duck." Especially if that man was Joshua Gardner.

"You're hopeless," Josie said, snapping her gum for emphasis.

"No, I'm a realist. And realistically there's no way Joshua Gardner and I will ever get along."

Joshua Gardner was a realist. Realist enough to know that working with Libby McGuiness—*Ms. McGuiness*—was going to be a huge pain. Either the woman didn't like men in general, or she just didn't like him. It didn't matter which it was—working with her was going to be a chore. He should have just let her bow out and asked Mabel to find someone else he could work with.

But he hadn't let her bow out.

In fact, he'd practically insisted she continue chairing the party. His actions didn't make sense. And if there was one thing Joshua Gardner liked, it was having things make sense.

Maybe that's why his breakup with Lynn had been so difficult. It didn't make sense. He'd thought they were happy…right up until the day Lynn told him she wanted a divorce. The divorce didn't make sense to Joshua, at least until he'd met Lynn's new boy-toy. Twenty-five with a washboard stomach. Then it made plenty of sense.

He looked down. His stomach wasn't exactly a washboard, but it wasn't potbelly, either. He took care of himself, but didn't push the line to obsessing about his body. And though he wasn't twenty-five anymore, he was happy being almost forty. Well, maybe not happy, but not dreading his forties. No midlife crises for him, unless you counted a failed marriage, and picking up and starting over again.

He'd been living the life that he'd always wanted… Well, except for kids. He'd wanted them. She hadn't. And they had none.

Lynn said she'd worked as hard for her degree as he had for his, and she wasn't about to give up all that work for some mewling brats. He'd pointed out he'd be willing to split the burdens fifty-fifty, just like he wanted to split the joys, but Lynn would hear none of it.

In the end, nothing was split quite fifty-fifty, but the

settlement was fair enough. Lynn had bought out his half of their practice, and it had given him enough to start over. To start here in Erie, his hometown.

Though his family had scattered throughout the country, this was still home.

So here he was.

Dr. Joshua Gardner of Gardner's Ophthalmology. Footloose and fancy-free, and utterly unsure of what to do with his loose ends.

He'd readily agreed to Mabel's request because chairing the Christmas party gave him something to do, and gave him a way to ease into the community he had joined. His agreement had nothing to do with the fact that the very bristly Ms. McGuiness would be working with him.

No. It had nothing to do with her at all.

She was his neighbor. This was just an excellent way to get over the hurdle of their first, inauspicious meeting.

That's all it was.

Chapter Three

A business meeting.

That's all this was.

People had them all the time.

The phrases ran through her head all day, and yet not one eased the raging case of nerves Libby had developed. It was only a meeting, and Libby didn't know why it was bothering her so much. But when she accidentally dropped her scissors for about the hundredth time of the day, she knew it was useless to deny her anxiety any longer.

She was nervous as hell about this little *meeting*.

"Would you stop fluttering around the shop like some sort of drunken butterfly?" Josie asked, exasperation in her voice. "He's only a man, sweetums. And men are a dime a dozen. You can take my word for that."

"He's not a man, he's a business associate. That's the only reason I'm seeing him tonight. Business."

"If you say so," Josie said with a sly smile.

"I do."

"Well, then settle down." There was more than a hint of indulgence in Josie's voice.

"I'm not nervous," Libby said with as much force as she could muster.

"Hey, my appointment just canceled," Pearly called as she came in from the back room.

"Why don't you just take off early?" Libby offered.

"That's one idea," Pearly said slowly.

Libby sensed a trap, but asked anyway, "What's the other?"

"You could let me have a go at that hair. It's getting so long, and it's such heavy hair that carrying around that weight all day can't be comfortable."

Libby grabbed her braid. No way was she going to let Pearly start *trimming*. "It's fine."

"Don't you trust me?" Pearly asked innocently. Much too innocently.

"Of course I trust you," Libby reassured her, even while she silently added, *As far as I can throw you.* "But I don't have time to get my hair cut. I have a meeting in an hour and have to close up the shop and—"

"We'll close up the shop for you. And I'm not talking a cut, just a small trim," Pearly pressed.

"You really need one," Josie said, blatantly choosing Pearly's side as she joined the skirmish.

"Well…"

"Come on, Libby." Pearly sensed the kill was at hand and pounced. "You just sit yourself in this chair and let me give your hair a quick rinse. We'll have it all trimmed, smart and proper, before your date—"

"It's not a date, it's a business meeting," Libby said again. Exactly who she was reminding she wasn't sure. She'd had meetings in the past and had never felt this jittery about any of them.

"Who's Libby meeting?" Mrs. Kane asked from Josie's manicure chair.

"The new doctor next door," Josie said.

"It's just a meeting," Pearly soothed. "Well, let's get this done before your *meeting* shows up."

Reluctantly Libby sat. The wash went fine, and Pearly led her to the chair, had the cape whipped over her shoulders before Libby could blink an eye. It wasn't until Pearly picked up the scissors that the trouble started. "Uh-oh."

"Uh-oh, what?" Libby asked, craning her head to peek in the mirror.

"I slipped with the scissors," Pearly cheerfully responded.

"How did you slip with the scissors when you've only just started?"

"It was easy. But don't you worry. You're going to just sit here and let me fix up this mess I created."

Knowing that her hacked hair was no accident, Libby resigned herself to a real cut—a cut she hadn't asked for and didn't necessarily want.

"Pearly, what are you doing?" she asked as the snipping seemed to continue for an inordinately long time. Libby cut hair for a living and knew that this was taking longer than a trim—even a trim with slipping—should take.

"You just sit back and relax. You don't relax nearly enough." Clip. Clip.

"And it doesn't appear I'm going to get much relaxing done tonight."

"Yeah, meetings aren't very relaxing, are they?" Pearly asked. Snip. Snip.

"Especially not when you're meeting with a handsome man like Joshua," Josie added.

Clip. Clip.

"I haven't met the new doctor yet." Mrs. Kane looked interested. "Is he that good-looking?"

"Better," Josie assured her.

"Worth getting an eye exam," Pearly added. Snip. Snip.

Clip, clip, clip.

"It sounds like a lot of cutting for just a small trim." Libby tried to turn and catch a glimpse in the mirror of what Pearly was up to, but Pearly grabbed her head.

"Well, there was that slip, remember." Clip. "But don't worry, you're going to love it." Snip.

"I already do," Josie piped in.

Libby groaned.

And when Pearly finally turned the chair so she could look at her *trim*, she groaned even louder. "Pearly!"

"I told you I slipped."

Muttering about scissor-slipping stylists, Libby toyed with her now-shoulder-length hair. It wasn't so bad, but she wasn't about to tell her sneaky, snipping, conniving employees that. She gave her head a small shake and watched in delight as the brunette curls, freed from the weight of her hair and her ever-present braid, bounced.

Despite the fact she didn't hate the cut, might even like it a bit, she wasn't about to admit a thing. She was just about to read them both a riot act when the bell over the door chimed merrily.

"Ready?" Dr. Gardner, the hunky reason for Pearly's slippage, asked as he walked through the door.

"Just let me get my coat." She grabbed it off the hook in the back room. Before she walked out the door she turned to the two haircut cohorts. "And don't forget to get in an hour early tomorrow for that little meeting we're going to have."

"What little meeting?" Pearly asked.

"The one where we discuss professionalism, honesty and nonslip scissors."

The phone rang and Josie practically vaulted over the chair to get it and escape the lecture.

"Nonslip scissors?" Dr. Gardner—Libby refused to think of him as Joshua—asked.

"Snips and Snaps," Josie said into the receiver.

"Private joke." Libby trudged after him toward the door. "Where are we going?"

"My place? I've got an apartment at Lovell Place, so it's close."

There was no way she was going to Joshua Gardner's home, no way at all. This was a professional association, and professional associations didn't get all chummy at each other's homes—dates did. And this wasn't a date.

"I was thinking maybe a restaurant, or—"

"Libby," Josie called. "It's Mrs. Henderson."

"Meg?" A sense of dread crept into Libby's heart. "Is something wrong with Meg?"

"She said there was a small accident."

A helpless feeling washed over Josh as the color totally deserted Libby. She raced for the phone, and he followed. Who the hell was Meg? A sister? A friend?

As she spoke in hushed tones to this Mrs. Henderson, some of the color returned to her face. By the time she hung up she looked better, though obviously still concerned. "Listen, I hate to cancel on you, but I've got to go."

"Who's Meg?" he asked.

"My daughter." With that she was gone and all Joshua could do was watch her leave.

Her daughter?

A hand touched her shoulder. "There's no husband to go with that daughter, if that's what you're wondering, boy."

He turned and looked into the graying stylist's warm eyes. "I'm sorry?"

"No, you won't be if you stick around. Libby's a woman no man would be sorry to have. And I said, she doesn't have a husband, leastwise, not anymore, so you don't have to look so puppy-dog sad."

"Miss—" Joshua left the word hanging, realizing he didn't know the woman's name.

"Missed a man, that's the only Miss I've got. And the name's Pearly. Pearly Gates. You see, the day I was born my mother—God rest her soul—took one look at me and said she was looking on a piece of heaven. She named me Pearly, Pearly Gates, to remind herself—and me, too—what I was."

Josh couldn't help but smile. Before he could make his escape, Pearly added, "And Mama used to say it was a good thing she named me Pearly 'cause she needed all the remindin' she could get. Seems I might have come from heaven, but the devil put his two cents in my makeup. I was always gettin' in one piece of trouble after another. Mama said the gray hairs on her head were all mine. I figure this—" she ran her fingers through her short gray hair ''—is her way of getting even with me.''

Pearly laughed, not a quiet ladylike noise, but a laugh full of all the gusto she had for life. ''And Miss cracks-her-bubble-gum over there is Josie. I can't think of an interesting story to tell about her.''

''Hey,'' Josie said, even as she blew the largest bubble Joshua had ever seen.

''Well, it's nice to meet you two,'' Josh said, not quite sure what to make of Snips and Snaps's two employees. ''And thanks for the information about Libby, not that it matters. We're just working on this Christmas party—nothing more, nothing less.''

''Okay,'' Pearly said, her tone saying she didn't believe a word of it.

''I just ended a marriage, left everything behind. I'm not looking for another relationship. The only thing I want from Libby is to get her to stop Dr. Gardnering me, and get to work on this Christmas party.''

''If you say so, sweetums.'' Pearly's grin said that she still didn't believe a word of it.

''I do say.'' Oh, he said, and then some. The last thing he needed right now, with the ink on his divorce decree barely dry, was a woman like Libby McGuiness, hard and as prickly as a hedgehog.

''Okay,'' Pearly said, pulling a pad of paper from a drawer.

''I'm not interested in Libby,'' he said louder.

''I believe you. You believe him, don't you, Josie?''

"Oh, yeah." Josie blew a gigantic bubble and it popped as if for emphasis.

"I'm not interested in Libby at all, except for getting this party planned."

"We heard you." Pearly began to scribble on the paper, seemingly forgetting Joshua was in the room.

Josie snapped her gum again. "We've got it, Dr. Gardner. You are not interested in Libby."

"Good. I'm glad we've got that straight."

"Of course, being a doctor, you probably want to head over to her house and see if her little girl is all right," Pearly said.

"I'm an ophthalmologist, not a pediatrician. I'm sure if there's a problem, Libby will call her own doctor."

"I'm sure you're right." Even as she said the words, Pearly ripped the piece of paper off the pad. "But just in case you're driving by her house on the way home, you might want to stop." She thrust the note at him.

"Thanks, but I don't think so." He stuffed the paper in his coat pocket. There was no way he was going to Ms. McGuiness's house to check on her little girl.

No way at all, he assured himself as he drove through town.

It wasn't his fault that Erie had changed and he got slightly disoriented, so instead of finding himself at Lovell Place he found himself on Wally Avenue.

Wally Avenue? What an odd name for a street. It

sounded too eccentric for Ms. McGuiness to live on. She needed a street with a more prim-and-proper name. Primrose Lane. Now that would be appropriate for prickly, prim Ms. McGuiness.

He parked in front of the small gray ranch house. At least he thought it was gray. Darkness came early in November, so the house could be pink or green for all he knew. All the houses sort of looked gray.

Arguing with himself over what color house Libby McGuiness and her daughter lived in was about as stupid as things got. Well, maybe not as stupid as stalking his prickly neighbor to her home. Now, that was stupid.

Why on earth had he taken the address from Pearly? Or better yet, why on earth had he followed her down-home advice?

He sat in his car trying to come up with some sort of answer to either question.

After about five minutes, he finally admitted that he didn't have a clue what he was doing in front of the maybe-gray house. But whatever he was doing, it looked as if it was going to involve getting out of his truck, knocking on that possibly gray house's door and checking on Libby McGuiness and her daughter.

Neighborly concern, he decided. It was only neighborly concern that had prompted this trip. And the fact that he might not be a pediatrician, but he was a doctor. If Libby's girl was injured, he might be able to help.

Yes. Neighborly, doctorly concern. Nothing more, nothing less.

"Nothing more than a small bump. I don't believe you were in as much pain as you told Mrs. Henderson." Libby tried to stare her daughter down, but Meg simply averted her eyes to the lecture.

She took Meg's face gently in her hand and forced her to look at her. "What's going on?" she signed.

"I wanted to meet your date, but you didn't bring him."

First Pearly and Josie acting like she was getting ready for the prom, and now her daughter. Didn't anyone understand that it was the new millennium? Men and women had business meetings all the time without it being a date.

"It wasn't a date," she said again. "I told you that."

"Sure." Meg reached out and brushed a lock of Libby's hair. "First flowers, then you get a haircut for a business meeting."

"I didn't set out to get a haircut. Pearly was supposed to just trim it, but her scissors slipped."

Meg rolled her eyes, her expression saying more than any words—or even any signs—could.

"It wasn't a date. And since I got called away, it wasn't even a meeting. He's an annoying man whom Mabel got to help me plan the Christmas party. He can't even park."

"Neither can you," Meg reminded her, pantomiming pulling a car forward, then reverse, then forward…

Libby grabbed Meg's hands to stop her. "Watch it. You're already on thin ice," she signed with a smile.

Meg's humor evaporated when she got down to what was really bothering her. "You planned your date so he wouldn't meet me. You were embarrassed." Meg averted her eyes, plainly not wanting to *hear* her mother's response.

Libby repositioned herself so Meg *had* to look at her. "I have never, never been embarrassed by you," she signed in hard, choppy signs. "You are the most important thing in my life. And you know you've planned on spending tonight at Jackie's since last week, long before I even met Dr. Gardner. That's the only reason I set up this meeting for tonight." Libby paused and then added, "And if it would make you feel better, I'll plan the next meeting so you can meet Dr. Gardner."

"He won't like me. None of them do."

It didn't surprise her that Meg realized the few men Libby had dated *had* been uncomfortable around her. Meg was a perceptive child. She was trying to come up with some response when the light flashed and the doorbell rang.

"I'll get it." Meg's lightning-fast fingers flew, almost as fast as her feet beat a path for the door.

Libby was right on her heels. This answering the door after dark had to stop. They lived on a nice street, in a nice neighborhood, but still, there were nutcases everywhere.

Meg threw open the door just as Libby skidded into the foyer. Neither said a word as they came face-to-face with Joshua Gardner.

Speaking of nutcases.

"Did you forget something?" Libby asked.

"Since you couldn't come to the meeting, I thought I'd bring the meeting to you and check on your daughter." He smiled. "Hi, I'm Josh."

Meg shot Libby a stormy look, and then marched out of the foyer and down the hall. Libby heard a door slam and knew Meg had shut herself away from Josh's reaction to her.

Libby wasn't any happier to see their unexpected guest, but barricading herself in her room wasn't much of an option. Josh Gardner was quickly becoming a thorn in her side, a truck in her parking place...a blur on her eye chart.

"I seem to set all the McGuinesses' teeth on edge," Josh muttered.

"I suppose you want to come in," Libby offered in her most ungracious manner.

"Listen, this was a mistake. I'm sorry to bother you. I just thought if your daughter had an accident, you might want someone to take a look and—"

"Oh, don't go all nice-guy on me. You'll ruin my image of you and I'd hate to have to change it." Libby moved back, allowing Josh entrance to the house. "Come on in."

"Your daughter's okay?"

"Oh, the call about the accident?" Libby shrugged as she started toward the kitchen. What she needed was a hot cup of tea to soothe her rather frazzled nerves. Scissors slipping, business meetings everyone thought were dates, and a ten-year-old daughter's insecurities—what a day.

"The call was a ruse. She didn't want me going out with you, even though I assured her it was just a business meeting."

"So, neither McGuiness female likes me."

Libby whirled around in the doorway to the kitchen. "Listen, Dr. Gardner. I know we got off on the wrong foot, and I might have just let it go, but..." Libby paused, unsure how to continue this confession.

"But?"

"But in case you hadn't realized it, this co-chairing the Christmas party is just Mabel and the gang's way of fixing me up."

"With me?"

He truly looked surprised, and Libby found that strangely soothing. "You."

"Oh." Josh paused a moment. "I guess I should apologize."

"For what, being good-looking and a doctor?" Libby nodded at a chair, turned back around and started the teakettle.

Josh settled himself at her table, looking quite at home in her tiny kitchen.

"Listen, I should be the one apologizing. I've been on my own for a long time, and Mabel and the rest of them seem to feel I need mothering. So instead of just one overbearing mom trying to run my life, I have an entire section of town."

"Gets to be a bit much?" He flashed her a sympathetic smile.

"Way too much sometimes. Times like this." Libby turned and pulled out three tea bags and draped them into the teapot. "I just wanted to set the record straight. I'm not in the market for a man, and I certainly don't want you to misunderstand what's going on. If you want to back out of working on the Christmas party, I'll understand." She tried to keep her enthusiasm for the idea out of her voice.

"How about we agree right up front that there's no backing out for either of us, and we'll also agree that neither of us is interested in anything more than planning the party? Maybe we can put our parking incident in the past, and even become friends. We'll just let the PSBA ladies keep throwing me at you, and you can just keep dodging and not catching, and we'll get on with the job."

"You don't have to be nice—"

"Regardless of what you think, generally I am nice. So let's forget about parking problems, busybody businesswomen, moody children and just plan a party."

Relief flooded Libby's system. Joshua was apparently right. He was nice...at least sometimes. She offered him a tentative smile. "I'm making some tea. You're welcome to some, or would you rather have something else? Soda, juice?"

"How about just some ice water?"

"You drink ice water in this cold?"

"I've been told I've got ice in my veins, so I guess that explains it."

For a moment, Libby thought she saw a flash of pain on Joshua's face, but it disappeared and was replaced by a small laugh so quick that she couldn't be sure.

"Listen, I ordered a pizza on the way home. If pepperoni and mushrooms are okay with you, you're welcome to stay. We'll make it a working dinner."

"Sounds good. Do you need to go check on Meg?"

Libby felt another shot of pain on Meg's behalf. They obviously had more talking to do about this issue, but it would wait until after Josh went home.

"No. She'll come out when she's ready."

"Fine. So do you have the lists Mabel said she had for us?" Josh asked, suddenly all business.

Half an hour later the doorbell rang and the light flashed. Libby was halfway to the door when Josh called, "Do you want me to take a look at your circuit breakers? The doorbell ringing shouldn't affect the lights like that."

"It's for Meg," Libby called back as she opened the door.

The pizza delivery boy took her money and handed her a box. "Thanks," she told him, and the mother in her demanded she add, "And be careful out there tonight. The roads are getting slick."

Wally Avenue was notoriously undersalted and underplowed. The guilt of a pizza boy sliding off the road just because she'd ordered dinner was something Libby didn't want to have to worry about.

"Thanks, ma'am, I will," the boy called as he walked toward his car.

"Dinner's here," Libby said, scooting the papers over to the side of the table and putting the pizza in the center. "Just let me go get Meg and we'll eat."

"You're sure she's going to want me here?"

"It's time Margary Rae McGuiness learns that the world does not revolve around her." Libby paused a moment, then added with a grin, "Only her mom does."

Josh watched Libby shoot down the hall. The last half hour had been productive and, if he was honest, almost pleasant. Libby's small kitchen with its bright yellow walls and cheery blue accents, seemed like home. It wasn't a thing like the very proper kitchen, proper house he'd lived in with Lynn. This kitchen felt lived in, rather than feeling like showcase.

And, when Libby McGuiness let down her prickly defenses, she was almost nice. They'd got off on the wrong side of the parking spaces, but maybe that was behind them and they could be friends, as well as business neighbors.

The tick of the kitchen clock and the hum of the refrigerator were the only sounds in the house. Josh wondered if Libby and her daughter were carrying on a hushed argument down the hall.

They rounded the corner, surprising him. Hands flying. Libby laughed at something Meg must have said, though the girl wasn't saying anything. She was using sign language.

Libby paused, and smiled at Josh. "Dr. Gardner, this is my daughter, Meg."

The girl's fingers stopped flat and she eyed him with obvious distaste.

Josh felt awkward, and gave a little wave of his hand. "Tell her I said hi."

Libby's hands flew and Meg shot him a look he couldn't interpret.

"Well, let's eat," Libby said in a rush. She signed as she spoke through the meal, managing to grab bites in between interpreting and conversing herself. At first Meg didn't respond at all, but slowly her hands became more animated, but Josh caught her casting glances his way, as if she was studying him.

The girl was deaf...hearing impaired, he corrected mentally. At first Josh was as uncomfortable as Meg appeared to be. He was unsure how to behave. No one had mentioned Libby's daughter's problem. Of course, that explained the flashing light—Meg couldn't hear a doorbell.

As the dinner wore on, and Meg relaxed, she signed about her day at school.

Libby casually repeated the words for Josh, and he began to feel more and more at ease. It would probably be considered politically incorrect to admit his initial discomfort. He wasn't sure how to act, and he hated feeling awkward. But, as the meal wore on, he began to realize he didn't have to act like anything but himself. Watching Libby and Meg together, listening to, and watching their chatter, Josh slowly began to see the little girl, not the handicap.

"And we started some stupid algebra thing."

"Algebra in fifth grade? I think I was still working on long division," Libby said.

"It's pre-algebra, working with fractions and equations. I don't get it."

Josh couldn't miss Libby's suppressed groan as she said, "I'll take a look later, but you know how good I am at math."

Watching Libby's look of martyrdom as she made the offer, he couldn't resist offering, "Or I could help."

"What?" Libby asked.

"Tell Meg I was always pretty good with numbers, and I think I can muddle my way through fractions and equations."

Libby shot him a skeptical glance, and then signed for her daughter.

Meg's eyes narrowed as she studied Josh. He could see her unenthusiastic reception of him warring with her need to understand her homework.

Slowly Meg simply nodded her head at Josh.

"You're sure you don't mind?" Libby asked.

"No problem." Libby was looking at him as though he'd just crawled out from under a rock. Just in case he was wearing leftover pizza, Josh swiped his hand across his chin. "Why don't you do the dishes, I'll help Meg and then we'll wrap up for the night?"

"Don't you need me to interpret?"

"I think we can manage with the pen-and-paper method of communicating." He shot her a grin, hoping to ease whatever she was worried about. "If I get stuck, I'll holler," he promised.

Still looking unsure, Libby shrugged. "Okay."

Josh followed Meg down the hall to her room, aware he'd puzzled Libby. And the fact that he puzzled her, puzzled him. Did she think the fact Meg signed would bother him? Okay, maybe he'd been a little uncomfortable at first, but it was a fleeting feeling that had more to do with unfamiliarity than anything else. Or did she still think he was a complete jerk?

Meg tugged on his sleeve and pointed to the open book on her desk.

Josh took the book and sat on the edge of her bed, quickly scanning the instructions. Then Meg handed him a paper with her problems on it and pointed to the one she was stuck on.

"You didn't add it to the other side, too," Josh said, then caught himself. He mimed a pencil and paper, and Meg dashed back to her desk and retrieved them.

She sat on the bed, keeping as much distance as possible between them as she watched him begin to write down the problem.

"You didn't add the five to the other side of the equation, too," he scribbled. "What you do to one side, you always have to do to the other. Watch." Meg inched closer.

Slowly Josh worked his way through the steps of the problem. "See?" he wrote on the scratch pad.

Meg nodded.

Josh pointed to the next problem and handed the book and homework sheet to Meg. He watched as she worked her way through the short equation. She was a bright girl, grasping the idea after just one example.

He nodded and smiled to let her know she had it, and then watched in delight as she rapidly worked the rest of the problems.

"Thank you," she wrote.

Josh took the pen and wrote, "You're welcome."

He rose to leave the room when Meg tugged on his sleeve and pointed to the pad. "Do you play video games?"

Josh nodded.

Meg walked over to the edge of the bed, and pulled

up a system. She pointed to the cartridge and raised her eyebrows. Josh didn't need to know sign language to recognize the invitation.

"You're on," he said, and took a control.

That's how Libby found them half an hour later, both merrily blowing up darting androids. She stood in the doorway and watched her daughter laughing and carrying on with Josh, as if they'd known each other for years, as if they weren't separated by a communication barrier. Actually, watching them, Libby couldn't see any barrier at all.

For all Meg's initial storminess regarding Josh, she was all laughter and smiles now. And Josh seemed to be enjoying himself, as well. She'd caught his initial discomfort and had seen as it rapidly faded.

Watching them, Libby realized how much Meg must miss having a man in her life. This is what Mitch could have been to his daughter if he'd stayed around past her toddlerhood. He could have learned that though Meg had one small difference, she was just a little girl who laughed and cried, who played video games and had trouble with algebra.

Josh looked up and spotted her. "I guess the kitchen's clean, huh?"

"Doing dishes after take-out pizza isn't all that tough," Libby spoke and signed at once without even thinking. "And since you two are busy blowing up the world—"

"Saving the world," Josh corrected her with a grin.

"Saving the world," Libby amended, "can I assume the algebra's been conquered?"

"Totally defeated, ma'am," Josh said with a salute that set Meg to giggling.

"Well, then Meg's got to get ready for bed, and you and I should wrap up the party planning for tonight."

"How do you say, thanks for the game and good night?" Josh asked.

Slowly Libby walked him through the appropriate signs. "You don't actually sign every word we speak. American Sign Language, A.S.L., has its own syntax. So you'd say this." She made the signs and Josh mimicked them. Meg grinned and slowly signed good night back at Josh.

He followed Libby back down the hall. "She's a great kid," he said softly.

"I think so."

"Has she been deaf all her life?"

Libby was startled by the directness of his question. Most people when they first met Meg skirted around the issue of her hearing impairment. But then, most people were also uncomfortable trying to communicate with Meg, and that hadn't seemed to bother Josh a bit.

"Meggie was premature, and for a while we weren't sure she was going to make it. No one's really sure if she was born deaf, though there's no history of hearing problems in either family, or if all the fevers and meds they used to save her injured her hearing. She was eight months old before we discovered she couldn't hear, and by then it didn't matter how she lost her hearing. It just mattered what we were going to do about it.''

''And what did you do?''

''Raged against fate, against God for a while and mourned the loss of the child I thought I was getting. The perfect baby I'd imagined. Once I let go of that image and really looked at the baby I loved so much, I realized how lucky I was.''

Suddenly realizing how much she was saying to this man who was practically a stranger, Libby added, ''Anyway, I signed up for sign language classes, started to find out what was available in Erie to help Meg, and then just got on with living and enjoying my daughter.''

''It must have been tough.''

''It's been tougher on Meg than on me.'' Before Josh could ask any more questions, Libby hurriedly said, ''I'll check into the St. Gert's banquet hall tomorrow. If that pans out, we're that much ahead of the game.''

''So, I guess we're done, huh?'' he asked.

''For tonight.''

Thankfully, Josh took his cue and grabbed his stack of papers and his coat. ''Thanks for dinner.''

''Pizza is one of my specialties.'' Libby smiled. ''And, Dr. Gardner?''

"I thought we'd gone past that?" he gently scolded.

"Josh," Libby corrected herself. "I just wanted to thank you."

"I signed on for planning this party, just like you did. Mabel and the rest of the PSBA should be thanking both of us." He grinned at her.

Rather than set her teeth, she found his smile infectious. "No, I mean thank you for Meg."

Josh shrugged. "Like I said, I've always been good with numbers."

"No, I mean for treating her like a normal little girl."

"Isn't that exactly what she is?"

Josh's look of confusion seemed real—he truly saw Meg the way she did, as a normal little girl.

He'd been right earlier when he said he was normally a nice guy. Actually, he was a very nice guy, not that she was going to tell him that.

"Yes. Meg's as normal a ten-year-old as they make. But most people take a while longer to discover that. So, thanks. She likes you."

"Despite the fact she didn't think she would?"

Libby nodded.

"And her mother? What does she think of me now?" He took a step toward her, crowding her.

Libby took a step backward, needing to distance herself from Josh. "I guess Meg's mother would say she likes you, too." She was surprised at how breathy her voice sounded to her ears.

"Despite the fact she didn't think she would?" Josh repeated softly.

"Well, let's just say, although your parking leaves a lot to be desired, you have other qualities that make up for it."

Good night, Josh signed.

"Good night, Josh." Libby fingerspelled his name.

He watched her finger movements with a quiet intensity. "You'll have to teach me that next time."

"Anytime," she promised, even though she realized that after they were done planning the Christmas party there would be no time. That would almost be too bad. When he wasn't being an arrogant pig, Joshua Gardner wasn't a bad guy.

Libby watched his truck ease out of her drive and head down the road.

Meg tapped her shoulder. "Is he gone?"

"Yes." Feeling foolish for staring after Josh like some lovelorn teenager, Libby shut the door and turned toward her daughter. "We still need to finish our talk."

"I'm tired."

Libby could sense stalling when she saw it, but she let it slide. Meg had seemed more comfortable with Josh, and maybe there would be no more problems with her planning the party.

"Did you brush your teeth?" Libby simply asked.

Meg nodded.

"With toothpaste?"

Meg shot off down the hall like a shot from a cannon. Libby couldn't help but smile. Joshua was more right than he realized. Meg was just a regular ten-year-old girl.

Chapter Four

Josh made his way home slowly. The roads had slick sections and he'd rather be cautious than slide off the road.

Cautious.

That one word summed up Libby McGuiness to a T. Cautious and wary. Was it just him, or did she distrust people in general? Or maybe was it just men? In that small bit of personal history she'd spilled, she hadn't mentioned Meg's father. Did he have anything to do with her wariness?

Toward the end of the evening Libby had almost seemed comfortable with him. Laughing as they worked. It had been a long time since he'd felt an easy camaraderie with a woman. Maybe that was just another reason he and Lynn's marriage hadn't made it—they'd stopped laughing together when they worked.

As a matter of fact, though they'd shared an office, they'd really stopped working together. They'd each wanted different things. He'd wanted kids, a home and family. And Lynn? Well, she didn't. They stopped talking about what they wanted and had simply worked side by side. They'd put their careers, their patients and their practice, ahead of themselves as a couple. And now they weren't a couple anymore.

They were two strangers who used to be together. Coldly indifferent to each other.

In just one evening he'd probably noticed more about Libby McGuiness than he had about Lynn in the last year. When had he stopped noticing? When had she?

Thinking about his failed marriage and Libby, Josh realized his interest in his co-chairman might have something more than business in it and that would have to stop. He wasn't ready for anything more than business with a woman.

Oh, maybe a casual date now and then. But he knew deep down that there was nothing casual about Libby McGuiness. She was the type of woman to inspire more than just an occasional date. And since he couldn't give her more than casual, he better let go of any thoughts of her laughter and her smile.

He'd better forget how once he chipped away at her tough exterior, he'd found a vulnerable, desirable woman. Thinking about how she'd talked about Meg, he also realized that though she tried to hide it, Libby had a lot of emotions just waiting for someone to set them free.

That someone could never be him. So Josh was going to be a gentleman and stop thinking about Libby. He wasn't going to think about her at all.

They'd plan the party like they'd promised, but that was it. Josh couldn't afford to spend any more time than necessary with the very uncasual Libby McGuiness—for both their sakes.

Libby had thought Josh would call, but he hadn't.

That was just as well. Thanksgiving was just around the corner and after that it was the Christmas season. Holly, ivy and haircuts. That was going to occupy her time for the next month.

Adding to the general holiday craziness, she still had this party to plan. St. Gert's was a go. She wondered if Josh had gotten a caterer. He hadn't called to say one way or another.

But then, she hadn't called him, either.

This was ridiculous, she thought with disgust. She was like a schoolgirl, wondering if she should risk calling a boy she had a crush on. Only, she wasn't a schoolgirl, and she wasn't calling a boy she had a crush on. She was a businesswoman and it was time she took care of part of that business.

Sneaking into the back room while Pearly and Josie were tied up with customers, she quickly dialed Josh's office number.

"Gardner's Ophthalmology," came a female voice.

"Hi. This is Libby McGuiness, next door. Could you leave a message for Dr. Gardner for me?"

"Just a minute." A country song crooned in her ear. Libby wondered if Josh had chosen the music, or if the receptionist had. She wouldn't peg Josh as a country fan—opera maybe, but not country. If she hadn't already given her name, Libby would have hung up. She absolutely did not want to talk to Josh, she just wanted to leave a message.

"Dr. Gardner."

"Um, Josh, it's Libby. I just wanted to leave a message and tell you that I got St. Gert's hall."

"Good. I was going to call you later and let you know that Colters is going to do the catering."

"Well, good. We're making headway." And the sooner they finished the party plans, the sooner Joshua Gardner was out of her life, and hopefully out of her thoughts.

"There are still a few things we need to go over."

"When?"

"Tomorrow night after work, at your place?"

The thoughts of Joshua in her home again, filling the nooks and crannies made Libby uncomfortable, but she knew she was being ridiculous. Meeting at her place was more convenient because she wouldn't need a sitter for Meg. "Fine."

"I'll see you at seven. Gotta go."

Libby held the phone and listened to the dial tone.

She'd see Josh tomorrow. Why was it her heart suddenly felt lighter than it had in days?

But it wasn't a light heart that beat in her chest the next day, it was the sinking realization that no matter what she said or did, Josie, Pearly and Mabel were going to keep throwing her at the new doctor, hoping he'd catch her, or at least patch her up if she fell. It was no coincidence that the matchmaking trio had decided to have a girls' night out with Meg.

Well, this was a business meeting, she assured herself as she glanced in the mirror and smoothed a stray hair. The sooner the Tiresome Trio recognized that Libby absolutely didn't see anything in Josh Gardner beyond a business neighbor, the better. Oh, she couldn't help notice that he was attractive, if a woman liked that spit-and-polished doctorly sort of look.

It wasn't that Libby minded suave and sophisticated, it was just that she wasn't interested in men, no matter how sweet their smiles were—and Josh's smile was certainly sweet, in a sexy all-male sort of way.

She had her business and Meg, a daughter who deserved her mother's full attention. That was enough to keep anyone busy. She didn't need, or want, a man cluttering up her life. She was used to doing things on her own and she liked it that way.

Determined not to treat the evening as anything more than two business people working together, Libby purposely dressed casually. Faded blue jeans and an old, well-worn sweatshirt. There was absolutely no way Josh could think she saw tonight as anything more than it was.

The fact that she was checking her newly cut hair in the mirror had nothing to do with Dr. Joshua Gardner, and had everything to do with the fact that unbraided hair needed extra attention. She wanted to look casual, not messy.

The fact that she jumped when the doorbell sounded had nothing to do with nerves. It was just that—she glanced at her watch—he was early. Five minutes early. He'd startled her.

"You're early," she said by way of a greeting as she opened the door.

"I left extra time because of the snow, but it wasn't as bad as the weatherman made it sound." He brushed the light coating of snow from his coat.

"Don't worry. That could change in a heartbeat." Libby glanced at the snow-covered walk, knowing she'd probably be shoveling it by morning.

"I grew up in Erie's winters. I know how fast the weather can change, especially in the winter."

Realizing they were standing in the open doorway talking about the weather, Libby stepped back. "Sorry, come in."

Josh stamped his sneakered feet on the porch before entering the house. He kicked his shoes off and left them in the entry before he followed Libby to the kitchen. She couldn't help but peek over her shoulder at his large shoes joining hers and Meg's. She couldn't remember the last time a man's shoes sat next to hers.

The image was disconcerting.

"You really should get some boots," she said over her shoulder. "Those sneakers won't keep your feet dry if the snow really kicks up."

"Yes, ma'am."

Libby could feel heat steal to her cheeks. "Sorry. The mom gene sometimes kicks in without my wanting it to." She nodded at the table. "Have a seat."

Josh slid into the same seat he'd occupied the last time, looking quite at home there. Like his sneakers sitting in her foyer, Josh reclining comfortably at her table was uncomfortable.

"Don't worry about the mom gene," he said with a smile. "It's been a long time since anyone's worried about me. It's kind of nice."

"I..." Libby wanted to assure him she wasn't worried about him, but the words would sound too harsh, so instead she switched to a safer topic. "Listen, like I said earlier, I called St. Gert's and we've got the hall for the weekend before Christmas."

"Great."

Rather than sit down opposite him, she grabbed her mug from the table. "Want some coffee before we dive in?"

"Sure."

Libby refilled her cup and poured Josh a mug before

they dove in feetfirst. Slowly, hardly aware that it was happening, Libby relaxed.

An hour and a half later, coffee mugs empty and party details all wrapped up, Josh stretched. "Wow. You're a slave driver."

Libby shuffled her stack of papers into an orderly pile and put them back into the file. "But it's pretty much all done."

"Except the shopping," Josh reminded her.

"Mabel gave me a list of kids' names and ages." She had the list somewhere in the file. She thumbed through the papers, looking for it.

"Why don't we go Friday? The day after Thanksgiving is some of the best shopping of the year—that and Christmas Eve."

Libby stopped short and glanced up, surprised at the offer. "Meg and I can handle that part." Shopping together the Friday after Thanksgiving had become an annual event.

"If I asked please, could I come along?" There was a little boy begging for a treat quality in the request.

"Why would you want to give up part of your long weekend at a toy store?"

Spending more time with Joshua wasn't the smartest move. He was... Well, Libby wasn't sure what he was, but she was pretty sure she preferred being annoyed by her new neighborhood ophthalmologist than feeling comfortable with him.

"I'm new in town, remember? It will give me something to do."

"Oh." She couldn't think of any valid reason why they couldn't all go together. Not one.

"So what if I pick you both up at about ten-thirty Friday morning?" he pressed.

"I guess that would be okay." Why did the idea of spending more time with Joshua bother her? They were working together on this project, so even though they were shopping, it was still business, nothing more.

"Don't sound so enthused at the prospect."

"Sorry." Libby smiled as she stood, ready for this evening to be over.

Josh rose and moved toward her. "Is it me?"

Libby, needing to keep some distance between them, stepped back until she was stopped by the counter. "Is it you what?"

He took another step, once again closing the distance between them. "Is it me that makes you so nervous, or is it men in general?" he asked softly.

"I don't know what you mean." *Was that her voice?* The husky sound was foreign to her ears.

"I think you do," he whispered, taking the last step that brought him directly in front of her, but not quite touching.

"Josh."

"You know, I sat here working tonight wondering…"

He reached out and traced her jawline, a whisper-light touch that left Libby yearning to ask for more, but knowing she shouldn't. "What were you wondering?" she asked instead.

"What it would be like to do this—"

His lips touched hers with a quiet introduction. Soft and tender, he tasted and explored. And as much as she knew she should pull away, for just one moment Libby allowed herself to answer his lips with an introduction of her own.

How long had it been since she'd lost herself in the wonder of being held, of being kissed like there was no tomorrow? Libby couldn't remember, but in a rush she did remember all the reasons she shouldn't be kissing Joshua Gardner in her kitchen.

She pulled back. "Josh, that can't happen again." Her voice was breathy, and even to her ears didn't seem to carry any weight of conviction.

"Why can't we, Libby? We're alone, we're adults and I think we both would like to let that happen again, and again, and—"

"Because I'm not looking for—"

"For what? For kisses in the kitchen?" Josh drew back and forced himself to treat Libby's rebuff casually, though there was nothing casual in the feelings that one kiss had sent cascading through his body. "It was just a friendly kiss, nothing to worry about. You could have stopped it at any time."

"I did stop it." Her eyes didn't meet his. As a matter of fact, she looked everywhere in the kitchen except for at him. Libby looked like a nervous deer, ready to bolt for cover.

"Not very fast," Josh pointed out gently, backing up and giving her some space. Libby may have stopped the kiss, but not before he got a taste of how sweet Libby McGuiness could be. Not before she left him hungry for more.

"I was too surprised at first to do anything." Her voice was a little stronger, now that there was some distance between them.

"Which is why you kissed me back? Because you were too surprised to do anything else?" Josh couldn't resist asking.

"I—" She stopped and said, "Okay, maybe I did kiss you back a little, but it was just a momentary lapse, one neither of us will be repeating."

"You're sure?" he pressed.

"Absolutely positive."

"All right." Josh would let her think that their kiss was a momentary lapse, but that didn't mean he wasn't going to try to see to it there were many other moments where they could try for a repeat performance.

"All right?" she asked, suspicion lacing her voice.

It was all he could do not to reach out and touch her again. Because the urge was so strong, and because he knew that Libby wasn't ready for more touching, which would certainly lead to more kissing, he turned and picked up his papers from the table.

"If that's what you want, Libby, I'm not going to push you."

A look of relief swept over her face. "That's good, because that's what I want."

Josh started toward the front door.

"You're going?" she asked.

"We're done here for tonight." Just for tonight, he added silently. Now that he'd tasted Libby McGuiness, he knew he couldn't promise her more than that. "I'll see you Friday at ten-thirty."

"You still want to go shopping with us?" she asked, sounding surprised.

"Libby, it was just a simple kiss," he blatantly lied, knowing there was nothing simple about that kiss, or about the way Libby affected him. "I think we both can manage to put it behind us and concentrate on the job at hand."

Was it just with him, or did she avoid getting close to men in general?

"Well, I'm glad you're not mad."

"Libby, it might be old-fashioned of me, but I believe when a woman says no, it means no." At least until she said yes again. And if she said no on Friday, he'd listen, but he hoped that she'd say yes—no, he hoped she'd say, *Oh, yes.*

"Well, I'm glad." She smoothed her sweatshirt, brushing her hand down it, as if she wanted to brush away any imprint he'd left on her body, as well. "I meant what I said. I'd like us to be friends. And I'll see you Friday. Let's make it seven instead of ten-thirty. The stores open early and beating the crowd is half the fun."

"Seven, then," he said as he walked out into the frigid night air. Friends. Libby wanted them to be friends. That should suit him just fine. He wasn't looking for anything more than that, either. He wanted nothing more than a friendly relationship with Libby—with any woman for that matter.

So he had no idea why he'd kissed her, or why her withdrawal from that kiss had felt almost like physical pain. All he knew was that kissing Libby McGuiness was something he should definitely avoid in the future. Josh also knew, despite his best intentions, that he wasn't going to be able to.

Again, Libby couldn't seem to leave the window until Josh's taillights had completely disappeared down the street. Shopping on Friday was just part of the party planning, that's all. Josh only wanted to go with them because he was new in town and had nothing better to do. She wasn't going to read anything more into the day.

He had moved back home and hadn't reestablished old friendships and hadn't had time to make any new ones. She wondered what he was doing for Thanksgiving dinner. She should have asked.

Her conscience stabbed at her—maybe he didn't have anywhere to go—but she ignored the small voice whispering in her mind. There was no way she was inviting Joshua Gardner to dinner. Pearly and Josie would just love that. If they cut her hair for just a business meeting, what would they do for a holiday meal shared with a man?

No, she wasn't going to feel guilty because there was no way she was going to invite Joshua Gardner, the kiss-stealing, parking-nightmare, alone-in-town doctor to dinner tomorrow.

No way at all.

Chapter Five

The next morning, Libby dialed the number she had now memorized, and actually let the phone ring once before she slammed the receiver back down. There was no reason on earth that she should be feeling guilty. That's what she kept telling herself, but *telling* and *feeling* were two different things.

She opened the oven door and basted the turkey. No reason at all to worry about what Joshua Gardner was doing for Thanksgiving dinner…all alone. No, she doubted he was all alone. He probably had some old friends he was eating with.

She'd never asked, but maybe he still had some family in the area. That made sense. If he grew up here, there was bound to be someone who would invite him over for dinner. It wasn't up to her to feed him.

She had all she could do to deal with Meg, Josie and Pearly.

Mabel was having dinner with her new boyfriend, so it was just for the four of them. And she knew *dealing* with was exactly what she was going to have to do since Josie and Pearly were probably going to spend the entire afternoon grilling her about last night's meeting—and it had been a meeting. That's all it had been.

Of course she didn't often kiss people she was meeting with. As a matter of fact, Libby couldn't remember the last time she'd kissed anyone other than Meg. And the feelings kissing Meg evoked weren't quite the same as the feelings kissing Josh evoked. Feelings that—

"Mom!"

If hands could yell, then Meg was absolutely shouting at her. "What?"

"I've been trying to get you to listen to me."

"Sorry, I was just thinking," she signed.

"Is something wrong with the turkey?"

Trust a child to worry about practical matters. Libby tugged on Meg's braid. "Not a thing, other than I'm worried that fifteen pounds might not be enough to keep you happy."

"I like turkey."

"You are a turkey."

"And you are out of it today. Josie wants to know if she can bring a friend to dinner."

"Josie's got a friend? I hadn't heard." It wasn't her most witty joke, but then Libby wasn't feeling overly witty today. Meg had hit the nail on the head—she was out of it. "We should probably check him out. Tell her sure."

"Okay. She's really getting the hang of the computer. She found me in my chat room. Have you seen her computer? It's three times as fast as ours."

Meg didn't need audible words to instill wistfulness in that last sentence. Libby deliberately tried to keep her face neutral. "I told you, there's no way we can afford a new computer for a while."

"I know." Ever mercurial, Meg suddenly grinned. "I'll tell Josie to bring her new guy along."

Libby watched Meg whiz down the hall, and turned her attention to crimping the pumpkin-pie crusts, as she thought about how surprised Meg would be when she saw the brand-new computer Libby had ordered for Christmas.

Thinking about computers and pumpkin pies was preferable to thinking about Joshua Gardner and his kisses.

Libby kept forcing her thoughts to the dinner at hand, but was relieved when the doorbell finally rang a little while later. Josie's new boyfriend would be more distracting than pies and computers.

"Josie, you made it. Where's your *friend?*"

"He's getting the green Jell-O salad from the car,"

Josie said as she breezed into the house. "It sure smells good in here."

"Thanks. Did Pearly come with you?"

"No, I drove alone." Josie handed a bowl to Libby and took off her jacket.

"But what about your friend?" Libby asked.

"Oh, he brought his own truck." She hung her coat in the closet. "He left it on the street—though how he squeezed his truck in that tiny little space is beyond me—so I could get into the driveway."

"Oh. So, what's his name?"

"Well, you see—"

"Hi, Libby. Thanks for the invitation." The look on Josie's face said everything the sound of Joshua's voice didn't.

"You brought *him?*"

"I am going to assume that your tone was enthusiasm, not annoyance," Josh said good-naturedly. "Do you mind if I put this stuff in the kitchen before I drop it?"

"You know where it is."

"Yes, I do." He pried his sneakers off his feet before heading into the kitchen.

"You brought him?" Libby repeated softly.

Josie had the grace to look worried. "He's new in town—"

"No, he's not. He's from Erie."

"—and didn't have a soul to spend the day with. Would you feel better if he was eating all alone in his unpacked apartment? I'd be surprised if the man even owned a set of pots and pans.''

"There are restaurants.'' Libby thrust the bowl back into Josie's hands.

"Libby, I'm surprised at you. Just what did he do to make you so hardened against him?''

Libby opened her mouth to explain, but then snapped it shut again. Mentioning the fact that he'd kissed her certainly wasn't going to quiet Josie and her two cohorts down. If anything, it would galvanize them into more blatant attempts at matchmaking.

"Nothing. I was just surprised to see him at my door. The way Meg talked, it sounded like you were bringing a boyfriend.''

"And who says I'm not Josie's boyfriend?'' Josh teased as he came back from the kitchen. Unburdened now, he took off his coat and hung it in the closet.

"Oh, you are sweet,'' Josie said, planting a thwacking kiss on his cheek.

Josh casually laid his hand across Josie's shoulders. "So you'll be mine?''

Josie snapped her gum, then said, "Sweetheart, a woman like me would wear you out.''

"Do you think Pearly would agree to be my date?'' he asked.

Josie just laughed as she walked back toward the kitchen.

"Looks like you're batching it, Josh.'' Libby's teasing sounded forced to her ears, but she hoped it sounded suitably casual to Joshua and Pearly.

"There's one other woman I could ask," he reminded her softly.

"I'm afraid she'd say no," Libby said quickly, maybe a little too quickly.

"You don't think Meg would agree to be my date, especially after I show her this?" He pulled a video game from his pocket. "I rented it for today."

Relief. That was the feeling that flooded her system, Libby assured herself. Forcing herself to keep things light, she said, "Oh, bring the right video game and you can probably convince Meg to do anything."

"Well, there you have it. I've got my date, and I think I'll go challenge her to a match while I leave you to your cooking." Obviously comfortably familiar with her home by now, Josh started down the hallway.

"You don't cook?" Libby called after him.

He turned and offered her a schoolboy grin. "Not if I can avoid it. But I will offer to pitch in with dishes."

"Don't make offers you might regret," Libby groused.

"I'm always sincere in my offers," Josh said softly. "Always."

"Then you're on...for dishes that is." Libby walked into the kitchen.

"What other offers has Josh been making?" Josie asked.

Libby turned back to the counter and plucked Josie's salad off it, opened the refrigerator and tried to make room for it. "I don't know what you mean."

"I might not be the sharpest scissors in the shop, but that doesn't mean I can't see what's going on right in front of my face." Josie reached past Libby and stacked the butter on top of a bowl, leaving a hole for the Jell-O. "And something is definitely going on between the two of you."

"Nothing is going on. We hardly know each other."

"But...?"

"Josie, you're imagining things. There is absolutely nothing going on between Joshua Gardner and me. I don't especially even like him. He's a parking-space-hogging, noncooking, Christmas co-chairing, man."

"Ah, darling, the only thing important in that list of Josh's attributes is the *man* part."

"Have you been sniffing nail polish again? The last thing I need is a man and his parts cluttering up my life." Looking for busywork, Libby opened the oven and basted the turkey again.

"Sweetheart, I always let my mind wander where it will."

"Into the gutter."

"Isn't that the door?" Josie asked sweetly.

"It must be Pearly." Libby shut the oven and went to open the door, wondering if Pearly was part of Josie's newest fix-Libby-up assault.

"Hi, sugar." The graying-haired woman waltzed into the house with the ease of someone with a guilt-free conscience. "It smells wonderful in here."

"Thanks." Libby eyed Pearly.

"Josie here already?"

"Josie and her guest," she answered slowly.

"Oh, Joshua made it, too?" She took off her coat and put it into the closet herself.

"Aha." Libby pounced. "You did know. I thought I told you and Josie no more setting me up."

"What on earth are you talking about? It's Thanks-giving. Of course I assumed you or Josie invited Joshua. Who would let a new neighbor, a man who has no family nearby, spend the holiday on his own?"

Libby felt embarrassed. "Oh."

Pearly patted her back. "Libby, sweetheart, you have to quit assuming we all lead our lives vicariously through you. You're a sweet girl, a wonderful boss, and we all love you, but, darlin', we have lives of our own. And that includes Josh."

Feeling duly chastised, Libby followed Pearly into the kitchen. It was going to be the longest Thanksgiving in history.

It was one of the longest Thanksgivings in history, Josh thought morosely. It wasn't that the meal wasn't good. It was. The turkey was juicy, the stuffing was sage and onion with no odd additions, the potatoes were whipped smooth... Yes, the food was great. The problem was two ladies who didn't seem to know when it was time to call it a night.

Josh wanted to get Libby alone. And though Pearly and Josie seemed to be throwing them together, they didn't seem to realize it would be better if they threw Josh and Libby *alone* together.

Josie and Pearly kept talking about getting up and leaving, but neither of them did. No, instead, after everyone had cleaned up from dinner and had dessert, the ladies suggested they play a game. And so Josh found himself sitting at the table playing their third game of Scrabble…the longest games of Scrabble in the history of the game.

If Josh could stop thinking about kissing Libby, he might have even allowed that the games were fun. But he couldn't stop thinking about the way she'd felt in his arms, the way her lips had felt against his. He wasn't looking for a relationship, but Josh was looking forward to trying to kiss Libby McGuiness again. Soon. At least as soon as he could get her to himself.

Meg signed something to Libby who patiently spelled something back to her with her fingers. Fingerspelling. Josh had looked it up last night on the Web, and had a copy of the alphabet now. He'd spent the morning practicing, and even if he did say so himself, he wasn't doing too bad. He could at least make all the letters and even remembered a few. If he learned them all, he'd be able to communicate with Meg, even if he couldn't sign.

"Hey, that's cheating," Josh exclaimed as he realized what Libby was doing.

"What?" Libby turned from Meg and looked at him—really looked at him for the first time that whole day.

It didn't take much insight to figure out Libby was hoping to forget all about their kiss. And in order to forget it, she planned to pretend that Josh didn't exist.

Josh had other plans, though. One of them was to remind Ms. McGuiness that he did in fact exist, and if it took getting her annoyed to make her realize that, well, he was willing. Actually, he'd discovered after their first car-parking meeting that an annoyed Libby McGuiness was an incredibly tempting Libby McGuiness.

"You just told Meg how to spell a word. If I was quicker, I'd tell you what word, but I did catch the *R* at the end."

"Calendar. I told her how to spell calendar." Her eyes narrowed. "How did you know?"

"Aha, I was right." He was gloating, but not actually about being right about the letter *R,* but about the fact Libby's face was flushed. She was noticing him, all right. "And I knew because I've been trying to learn the manual alphabet. Unfortunately, although I can spell calendar, too, I don't think I'm quite up to your speed."

Slowly, laboriously he spelled the word. Meg clapped and made a sign.

"What did she say?" he asked Libby.

"She said good job."

Thank you, Josh signed back, another online piece of information he'd picked up. "And telling her how to spell a word is cheating."

"She's ten, Josh."

"So?"

"So, helping a ten-year-old who is competing against adults isn't cheating, it's…it's evening the odds."

Josie cleared her throat.

Josh watched in fascination as Libby's face colored even more. "Sorry," she mumbled.

"For what, Libby? Arguing with Josh in front of us? It's not us you have to worry about, it's poor Meg," Josie said as she signed.

"You know, it's important for children to learn to get along. How can the child learn how to behave like an adult if you go around forgetting we're all here and having a private argument with Josh?" Pearly asked slyly.

"I didn't forget you two were here," Libby blustered.

Josh sat back and watched the three women, their hands flying. No that wasn't quite right. He mainly watched Libby. She was back to being prickly, but the more he watched, the more he was sure he liked her prickly side.

Hell, who was he kidding? He liked all of Libby McGuiness's sides.

He noticed Meg was giving him a little wave, and he raised his eyebrows in a silent *what?*

The girl discreetly pointed at her mother, who was still sniping back and forth with Josie and Pearly. Meg slowly fingerspelled *L-I-K-E-S,* then made a motion that Josh assumed was the sign for like, and then pointed to Josh.

Josh discreetly pointed to himself, signed *like,* then pointed to Libby and Meg. Then he pointed to Meg, signed *like* and then pointed to himself, hoping she knew it was a question. When she nodded yes, Josh grinned.

"What are you doing?" Libby said, suddenly pulling Josh's awareness back to the rest of the Scrabble company.

"I just told your daughter I liked her."

Almost everything Libby said she signed, as well, but this time she said, without signing, "Don't mess with my kid, Gardner."

Suddenly the mood at the table changed. Pearly and Josie stopped teasing Libby, and Libby froze as solidly as Lake Erie in February. All the while Josh tried to understand what had just happened.

He liked Meg? Well, who wouldn't? She was a great kid. He envied Libby for having a daughter like her. He'd wanted kids so much, but Lynn hadn't. But if they'd had a kid, he wouldn't have minded a little girl with a contagious grin like Meg had.

Unfortunately, Meg's mother wasn't wearing any grin. She was scowling as she went back to the game. All four adults put on a pleasant front, but the Scrabble tournament wrapped up in record time. Pearly and Josie followed Meg back to her room to see something, leaving Libby and Josh alone, which was just what he'd been wishing earlier. But now, being alone with Libby felt awkward.

"I suppose you have to be going?" she asked hopefully.

"First I want to know what that little scene at the table was about?"

"What scene?" she asked innocently, much too innocently. She avoided looking at him again, this time by cleaning up the Scrabble game.

Josh sighed. Back to square one. He placed a hand over hers, halting the tile-picking-up process. "Libby, talk to me."

She pulled her hand back as if his touch had burned.

"What was the don't-mess-with-my-daughter scene all about? I simply said I liked her."

"No, that's not all you did. You went ahead and learned to fingerspell somewhere—"

"I said I surfed the Internet."

"And then you told her you liked her."

"I do like her. Meg's got a lot of spunk, not unlike

her mother, whom for the record, I said I liked, as well.''

"To who?'' Libby asked, a panic quality to her voice.

"Who did I say I liked you to? To Meg.''

"Don't.'' One cold, flat word—that's all Libby offered.

Softly, sensing there was more going on here than he could absorb, Josh asked, "Don't like you, or don't tell your daughter I like you.''

"Either. Listen, Dr. Gardner—''

"Josh.''

"You're my new neighbor. We're planning a Christmas party together. I'll even allow that you're not as obnoxious as I originally thought, but that doesn't mean I like you.''

"I never said you did, but I like you.'' What was going on here? Josh didn't want to get involved with anyone—he was still recovering from his divorce. What was Libby recovering from, or better yet, what was she running from?

"Don't,'' she said simply and stood.

Josh sprang to his feet, as well, and caught her by the arm before she could bolt.

"Libby, you can't just command someone to not like you. I like your spunk. I like the way you handle your daughter. I like the way you treat three interfering ladies who are obviously going to keep throwing us together. And I'll confess, I like them for the throwing.

But most of all, I liked the way you felt in my arms last night."

"I want you to forget about that." She squirmed, trying to break away from him, but Josh held tight.

"I can't forget any more than I forget how much I like you, and how much I'm wishing you had some mistletoe up."

"It's Thanksgiving—too early for Christmas decorations." She squirmed harder.

"I don't think it's ever too early for mistletoe. Personally I'm all for making it a year-round decoration in every house—especially yours." He released his grip on her arm, but before she could make her break, he wrapped her in his arms.

"Josh," Libby warned. Her squirming stopped and she froze in his arms, no longer fighting, but not relaxing, either.

"Libby, you know you've been wondering if it will be as good the second time." He removed one arm from her waist and raised his hand to trace her jawline.

Libby shuddered and momentarily leaned toward him. Then, as if she realized what she'd done, she jerked back as far as she could. "I'm not wondering anything of the kind. I don't want a second kiss."

Josh continued to hold her, but allowed her the space she seemed to need.

"You're lying," he said softly. "And to be honest, I can understand that. You don't want to like me, I don't want to like you. You don't want to want to kiss me. I don't want to want to kiss you, either. And yet, there it is. This feeling of like and respect I have for you, and this great big kiss, just begging to be had.''

"That was the most convoluted sentence I've ever heard," she snorted.

Josh dropped his arm from around her waist and Libby took a couple of steps backward, putting distance between them.

"How do you say *to kiss* in sign?" Josh asked.

"Josh." She took another step back.

"Do you just pucker up your lips and mime it?"

"You don't need to know how to say to kiss in A.S.L., or in English since we're not kissing again."

"How about French? I think it's *embrasser*. Did you ever notice that just about anything sounds better in French? *Embrasser*. I mean would you rather eat *escargot*, or snails? And would you rather *embrasse-moi* or kiss me?" Josh took a step in her direction.

Libby countered it. "I'd rather eat snails than *embrasse* you."

"Again, I say, liar. It's time you stop lying and start—"

"Kissing? I don't think so. You can take your over-inflated ego and go home. You said you understood last night. You said we could be friends."

"Libby, I said *if* that's what you wanted I wouldn't kiss you again, but it's not what you want. You want a kiss."

"Go home, Josh."

"Libby." He didn't want to leave her. The realization was a bit of a shock. As much as he'd been fantasizing about kissing her, Josh could rationalize that. After all, it had been a long time since he'd been attracted to a woman. Since he and Lynn had separated, Josh hadn't wanted any woman.

Now there was Libby, standing there with her extremely kissable lips. Right now those lips were tight with annoyance...or was it fear?

"I don't need anyone telling me what I want, what I think," she said. "I'm not afraid of you, I'm just too discerning to go around kissing parking-space-hogging egotists."

"I thought we were past the parking incident."

"And I thought we were past this kissing nonsense, but I guess we were both wrong. Good night, Josh."

Libby watched as, without another word, Joshua Gardner picked up his jacket and left.

There, she'd done it. She'd rid herself of the uninvited, kiss-stealing ophthalmologist. She was thrilled. Absolutely overjoyed that she'd finally made him understand that she wasn't interested. Yep, she was thrilled, she assured herself as she stood at the window, once again watching until his truck was out of sight.

"Good golly Miss Molly, you two got it bad," Pearly muttered from behind her.

Libby whirled around. "Got what bad?"

Rather than answer the question, Pearly said, "Your

fighting made the Thanksgiving feel like a real down-home holiday. That ruckus made me feel like I was back in Buford and Papa's pounding on the door for Mama." Pearly chuckled.

"Pearly—"

"Did I ever tell you about those two? They fought like cats and dogs—but they'd make up for hours. They'd send us all outside to pick berries, rake the yard or...well they'd think of some excuse and then...the ruckus they'd kick up. It took some growing up before we all realized they weren't still fighting."

Libby smiled in spite of herself. The world could be crashing down at her feet and Pearly would find a way to make things look brighter. Her down-home stories of growing up in the South grew and altered like the passing of the seasons, but they were always interesting.

"For once in her bubble-popping, polish-sniffing life, I think Josie's right. You and Josh are a great match."

"How can you say that? Every time we're together we end up fighting." That is when they didn't end up kissing, she silently added.

"Now, Libby, honey, if you and I can ever find men who fight like my father did and makes up just as wildly, well, I guess us two old spinsters had better just snap him up." Pearly tossed her coat on and opened the door. "Thanks for the dinner, and for making it seem like home. You just think on what I said."

Snap Josh up?

Ha!

There was no way Libby was going to have anything at all to do with Joshua Gardner once this Christmas party was over.

HOLLY JACOBS

Spent was missing Libby. Was going to have differ... dressed at to do wo... ...tcom Outback when the Christmas tree was there.

Chapter Six

"Mom, he's here," Meg signed just before she sped out of the room.

Libby purposely finished folding the last two T-shirts that she'd taken from the dryer. She'd started the load as soon as she woke up and wasn't in a hurry to finish since there was no doubt in her mind who the *he* Meg was referring to was. And though Meg might be brimming with excitement at the thought of the day to come, Libby didn't share her enthusiasm. *He* could wait a minute.

Actually, Libby had been hoping that *he* wouldn't show up, but she should have known *he* wouldn't back out of the shopping trip.

Joshua Gardner seemed to enjoy making her life miserable. Hogging parking spaces, showing up at

Thanksgiving dinner…kissing her. And most annoying of all, *not kissing* her.

Her hands stilled mid-fold. If she was honest, there had been a slight disappointment when he hadn't kissed her last night. She'd never thought of herself as a woman who said no and meant yes, but despite all the no's she'd said to him, all the times she'd denied it to herself, Libby had enjoyed their kiss the night before Thanksgiving and had felt a small pang of regret it wasn't repeated last night.

The feel of his body had imprinted itself on hers, and his kiss— She brushed her fingertip across her lips. How had such a small, tender kiss left her so at loose ends?

It had to be a hormonal reaction. It had been so long since Mitch had left, so long since anyone other than Meg had touched her, that her body had experienced a surge of hormones that had taken over momentarily. And now the moment was gone.

Libby was her rational self again—rational enough to know that there would be no more kissing between her and the very kissable Dr. Joshua Gardner. She'd resisted last night with no problem at all. Well, hardly any problem.

The fact that she'd spent a restless night, tossing and turning, had more to do with all the things that had to be accomplished in the next few weeks. The Christmas rush at Snips and Snaps, the Christmas party she'd been conned into planning and the shopping. She had to learn enough about megs and RAMs and modems to deal with Meg's computer. Those were the thoughts that kept her up last night. It wasn't thinking about Josh's kiss.

Her fingers brushed her lips one more time. No, she was totally over Josh Gardner and his very kissable lips.

"Libby?"

She whirled around guiltily, half-folded shirt in her hand and fantasy broken. Ignoring her racing heart, she forced herself to smile. "Josh. You're here. I'll, um, well I'll be ready in a minute. Almost done here."

"No hurry," he said. "Meg pointed me in this direction and then sped down the hall to her room."

"She's planning to do some of her own shopping today, and I imagine she's checking that she's got every cent from her various banks."

"What is she shopping for?"

"A new video game." Video games? She was standing talking to Josh about video games. It seemed a silly subject, but then Libby would welcome just about any silly subject if it meant they weren't talking about kissing.

"Maybe I'll stand a better chance at beating her if we're playing something new."

Libby wanted to warn him that after they wrapped up the party plans, he wouldn't have an opportunity to be playing anything with Meggie, but she didn't have a chance because Josh continued. "Why don't I go see if Meg's found all her money and we'll meet you in the truck when you're finished here?''

"I'm done now," Libby muttered to herself, since Josh was already gone. With all the enthusiasm of a prisoner marching to the firing squad, Libby plodded after Josh and Meg to the truck, which was practically pressed against her garage.

"Could you have parked any closer, Gardner?"

"Don't start on my parking again, McGuiness. I park just fine."

She snorted her response.

"This should go fast," she said as she took the giant step required to climb into Josh's huge truck.

Fast was definitely not the word to describe their shopping progress. Going through a toy store with Meg, especially when she had money, was never a treat. Meg would debate the merits of each potential buy, weigh her options and basically stall for as long as possible. Libby figured it couldn't get any worse.

But she was wrong.

Shopping with Josh and Meg was a lot worse.

Using her as an interpreter, they weighed the possibilities of each gift for each child on the PSBA's list. Two and a half hours later, sure that the worst was behind her, all that was left was Meg's shopping.

"But Quest is more money," Meg protested. "And Annihilator has more characters."

"Less graphic quality," Josh argued.

"Stop," Libby signed and said simultaneously. "No Annihilator. It's far too violent."

"I don't want a baby game," Meg signed, pointing at the educational Quest in Josh's hands.

"Not a baby game, but something with a little less blood and guts," Josh promised.

Meg didn't need Libby to interpret her violent head shake.

"How about this?" Josh asked, holding aloft Star Lords. "My friend Charlie has this, and I've played. Tons of action, no blood and guts."

"Will you play with me?" Meg asked.

Libby paused before interpreting. She didn't like it that Meg seemed to be growing so attached to Josh. Their homework/video bonding the other night, yesterday at dinner and now, shopping, chatting and laughing with him. Meg's attachment probably had nothing to do with Josh as a person. It was more Meg's longing for a man—any man—in her life.

"Mom," Meg signed.

"Sorry," Libby signed back even as she repeated, "Meg wants to know if you'll play with her," to Josh.

"If your mom invites me over when we're done shopping."

Libby glared at Josh, even as she signed the words, and added, "You're invited," as unenthusiastically as she could manage.

But her lack of enthusiasm didn't seem to dissuade

Josh at all. He just grinned and said, "Then, yes, I'll play."

"Okay." Meg happily put the game in the cart and pushed the overflowing cart toward the cashier.

"You didn't have to use my daughter to get an invitation over."

Josh laughed. "You mean you were going to invite me on your own?"

"No," she grumbled, wishing Josh didn't look so darned cute when he smiled. It just wasn't fair that one man should have so much appeal.

"Is this still about our kiss?" he asked softly.

"Shh. Meg can lip-read a little."

"But unless she has eyes in the back of her head, I don't think she managed it right now." His hand gently touched her shoulder. "So, is this awkwardness about last night's attempted kiss, or about our actual kiss the night before?"

"What kiss?" Libby asked. Why did their conversations always seem to circle back to kissing? Even worse, why did all her thoughts circle there, as well?

Libby McGuiness was a calm, rational person. What was it about Josh that left her skittering from one emotion to another?

"You can try to ignore our kiss, and I can try, but I think eventually we're going to have to try it again."

"Not if I can help it." Lagging farther and farther behind Meg, she stopped. "Listen, Josh, you're a nice guy, but I'm not looking for any guy, not even a nice one."

"I thought I was…what was the word? *Arrogant?*"

"Oh, you are, but you're also nice," Libby admitted grudgingly. "We agreed we'd just be friends."

Slowly Josh shook his head. "No, as I recall, you suggested it and I didn't fight it."

"Which is the same as agreeing." She took back the *nice* part. Josh was an arrogant, annoying man.

"In what court of law?"

"Mine. The only one that matters in this instance."

"Listen, Libby, you're not looking for a relationship. You've made that clear. I'm not, either. I just walked away from a marriage and I haven't even begun to figure out why it failed."

"You're divorced?" The question slipped out, and Libby wished it could slip right back in. Why did the thought of Josh and someone else disturb her so much? She didn't want him to read anything into the question. "Never mind, it's none of my business."

"Maybe it's not, but I'll answer anyway. Yes, I'm divorced. The marriage was over a long time before the papers were actually signed. Toward the end, it was more business than anything else. And like you, I'm not looking for a new relationship."

"But the kiss?" she asked.

"That's just it—it was just a kiss, Libby. I didn't pledge my undying love. Neither did you."

"So the kiss was just a momentary lapse of judgment on your part, too?"

"I don't know if I'd call it a lapse in judgment, but a kiss isn't a relationship. Two adults can kiss *and* be friends, Libby."

Meg was in line, waving wildly. Josh and Libby hurried to catch up.

"And they can be friends and avoid the kissing," she argued.

"If I try to avoid the kissing, can we try to get back to trying to be friends?"

"No kissing?"

He shook his head. "So, we're okay?"

"We're okay. And since you're going to be busy playing a game, I guess I could even ask you to stay for Thanksgiving leftovers for dinner."

"I thought you'd never ask."

"Neither did I," she admitted softly.

As she watched him in line with her daughter, grinning as they unloaded the gifts from the overflowing cart, Libby's fingers lightly brushed her lips. Their kiss was just a momentary fluke, not to be repeated. It had been a kiss, just a kiss, not a lifelong commitment. What had she been worried about? She should be relieved that Josh had agreed no more kissing.

So why was it that she wasn't?

"The video game is separate from the rest of the toys," Josh told the cashier as they reached the front of the line.

"No problem," the woman said, scanning the video game's bar code. "That's $45.72."

Before Libby could sign for Meg, Josh had simply held up the appropriate fingers for her. Libby could have told him that numbers in A.S.L. were slightly different than the way the general population made numbers on their fingers. A seven was the ring finger held against the thumb on one hand, rather than five fingers on one hand and two on the other. She could have told him that this allowed people signing to make any number on just one hand.

But she didn't say a word, because watching Josh interact so casually with Meg was causing something in her chest to constrict in a most unusual fashion.

After the cashier had handed Meg her change, Libby started loading the rest of the toys onto the belt, watching them slide to the scanner, which beeped merrily.

"I'm glad I'm not paying this bill," Josh joked.

Libby was about to agree when the cashier teased, "These aren't all for your little girl?"

"We're not—I mean, Meg's my little girl, but he's just a…"

"A what, Libby?" Josh asked quietly.

"A friend," she filled in.

"Oh, I'm sorry," the cashier said, and then fell silent as she ran myriad toys through the scanner.

Libby wasn't sure if the cashier was sorry she'd

made the mistake, or sorry that Libby and Josh weren't anything more than friends.

The look her *friend* shot at her wasn't very comforting. When the bill was paid and he pushed the overflowing cart out the door, he seemed almost angry.

"Is something wrong?" Libby asked.

"You tell me," was his curt retort.

"I'm sorry if the clerk thinking we were a family made you angry. It wasn't as if I had any control over what she thought."

"It wasn't what the clerk said, Libby."

"Then what?"

He shook his head. "Never mind. Let's get these all in the truck and get them back to your house."

The ride home from the mall might have been awkward if Meg hadn't kept up a happy stream of chatter, chatter Libby dutifully repeated for Josh's benefit.

"And Kari didn't have her homework done again, so Ms. Ross sent home a note. I never get notes because I always do my homework. And Ms. Ross said I should tell you Mercyhurst Prep is having a Christmas party for hearing-impaired kids again this year. I'm invited. The paper's in my book bag."

"Do you want to go?" Libby asked, still speaking out loud so Josh felt as if he was part of the conversation. She'd spent so many years making sure Meg felt connected, that making sure Josh was part of things was second nature.

"Sure," Meg said enthusiastically. "They have

cookies and it's fun to talk to the kids. The high school kids sign slow, but they try real hard.''

"Okay."

"Why does the high school have a party?" Josh asked.

"They have wonderful Sign Language classes and a Sign club. The club has special events for the hearing-impaired community, a way for the Mercyhurst students to get to try their signing in real-life situations. They even run a summer day camp for the kids. It's a nice program. Meg and a lot of her friends go, though the kids running the program change every year."

"We're allowed to bring someone to the party," Meg said.

"I know. I went last year, remember?"

"Maybe this year Josh would like to go with me." Libby repeated Meg's words without even realizing her daughter was inviting Josh until the words were out of her mouth.

"Meg wants me to go?" Josh asked.

Libby ignored his question and signed to Meg without repeating the words. "That's rude to put Josh on the spot. He doesn't sign and it might be uncomfortable for him to be surrounded by people he can't talk to."

"Some of the Mercyhurst kids aren't great at signing, but some are real good and they can interpret. He's not uncomfortable with me, even if he doesn't sign. He helped me with my homework and is good at video games, for an old guy.''

''Aren't you the one who didn't want me to date him?'' Libby signed, but didn't repeat out loud.

''Most of the guys you've dated don't like me.''

''I never date them long enough for them to know you—''

''You don't date them because they don't like me. I make them uncomfortable.'' Meg paused a moment, then added, ''Josh was uncomfortable that first night, but he's not now. He sees *me,* Mom. He doesn't see a deaf girl.''

''You're more than that.''

Meg nodded. ''We know that, but not everyone else does.''

It broke Libby's heart that her daughter sounded so much older than any ten-year-old should. She tried to protect her, but Meg was too perceptive not to notice how people reacted to her.

''Ask him,'' Meg said.

''I don't think it's a good idea,'' Libby insisted.

''Please. Ask him.''

''Josh, I'm sorry. We both realize that spending a day off with a bunch of Christmas-hyper kids isn't your idea of a day off.''

''I'd love to.'' Josh didn't even glance her way, but kept his gaze glued to the road. He was polite enough not to mention the entire conversation he'd been left out of.

"Really, you don't have to—"

"I don't have to do anything, Libby. Like I said when I agreed to plan this party with you, I haven't yet reconnected with anyone in town. It would be fun to get out with a bunch of Christmas-hyper kids."

"Josh—"

"I like kids. It was just one of the hurdles in my marriage. I liked kids, wanted them, but my wife—my ex-wife—didn't want them."

"I'm sorry."

He took his eyes off the road long enough to glance at her as he said, "So am I. Spending time with Meg has reminded me of how much I've missed out on."

"But that doesn't mean you have to go to this party with her."

"I want to. Unless you have a problem with me taking Meg. I realize we haven't known each other very long and you might not be comfortable—"

"That's not it."

No, Libby trusted Josh with Meg. Maybe there was no rational reason for that trust, but it was there. He'd never do anything intentional to hurt her daughter. But it was the unintentional pain that worried her. When the Christmas party was over and he walked out of their lives, Meg could be hurt. She tried to explain that to Josh. "It's just—"

"Just what?"

"Just that Meg and I are used to doing things on our own. I don't want her to come to count on you being around when in reality as soon as Christmas is over, you won't be.''

"We may not have a party to plan then, but we'll still be neighbors.'' He pulled into their driveway and cut the engine. He looked at Libby, looked at her with an intensity that stole her breath. "Just tell her I'd love to go, Libby.'' Her name on his lips was like a caress, intimate and tender.

"He said yes," Libby signed.

Meg didn't say a word, just turned and hugged Josh. Libby crawled out of the truck and handed a couple bags from the back to Meg, who trotted up the sidewalk.

"I guess that means she's happy," Josh said.

"Yes, *she* is." Libby could see how attached Meg was getting to Josh. What would happen when he left? And he would leave. Of that she had no doubt.

"Libby, what's this really about? I don't think it's Meg.''

"It is all about Meg, everything I do is about Meg. Becoming attached to you is a mistake. You're here now, playing the benevolent friend, but you'll be gone soon, and I'll be left to pick up the pieces." She grabbed a bag and marched into the house.

Josh trailed after her. No matter what Libby said, he didn't believe it was his friendship with Meg that was bothering her, worried that sooner or later he'd hurt Meg. No, Josh was pretty sure that it was Libby just waiting for him to hurt her.

That's why she reacted too strongly to his kiss, to his attempted follow-up kiss. She was afraid.

Dammit, didn't she see that he was afraid, too? He was just beginning to feel whole and healthy. He'd moved on, picked up the pieces of his life, packed up his practice and moved on. He was thirty-eight, dangerously close to forty, and trying to build a new life for himself. Becoming involved with anyone right now wasn't in his game plan.

And yet, every time Libby's blue eyes gazed at him, all his plans fell away and all that was left was the certainty that he wanted to know this woman better.

He wanted to know the woman who had managed to run her business and care for her daughter so competently. A woman who could crackle with anger over a bad parking job, and forgive just as easily. A woman who seemed to collect lonely people, and who with a simple smile, could make them feel as if they were part of something, as if they weren't alone anymore.

Libby might not understand it yet, but he wasn't about to walk away from the woman whose kisses awoke feelings in him that he thought had died long ago.

Maybe these feelings were what was missing between him and Lynn. He'd thought they had a good relationship, a companionable one full of shared interests and goals. But he couldn't remember the last time one of their kisses had affected him the way Libby's had.

He reached the truck and took out the last bag. "That's it," he said, carrying it back to the spare room Libby was using as the Christmas party storage space.

Meg's hands gyrated, and Libby sighed.

"What?" Josh asked.

"She wants you to come try out the game."

"And what do you want?" he asked softly.

"Oh, go play the game and I'll start dinner." She signed at Meg.

Libby started toward the kitchen, but Josh reached out and took her wrist, stopping her. "The invitation still stands?"

She jerked herself free from his grip. "I guess."

"Oh, Libby, you really shouldn't be so enthusiastic. Of course I'll stay for dinner. Heck, I'll even do dishes. Tell Meg she has to help."

Libby dutifully signed, and Meg, the same child who complained about any household assignment, said, "Sure, I'll help Josh." Meg grabbed Josh's hand and dragged him toward her room and the game.

Libby watched them go down the hall, her heart aching. Meg was getting too attached to the man, after only a few visits. How would Meg feel when he was no longer around?

She opened the cupboard and took out dishes. Left-overs required no cooking, so all she had to do was set the table, and take out the leftovers. If Meg or Josh wanted something hot, they could nuke it.

She automatically pulled out three plates. Three.

Having Josh at her table was becoming a regular thing. She couldn't allow that to continue. She'd told Josh they could be friends, and maybe they could, but she didn't plan to let this particular friend move in and start messing with her daughter, because Meg would be hurt when he was no longer there.

And as she told Josh earlier, Libby would be left to pick up the pieces.

"Damn," she swore as she dropped a plate. The pieces lay shattered at her feet and she knelt to pick them up. Yes, when Josh left, she'd be doing this all over again. Only, instead of some dinner plate, she'd be picking up a little girl who was desperate to have a man in her life.

Josh came skidding into the kitchen. "What happened? Are you okay?"

Libby didn't look up from the floor, just continued to pick up the pieces as she said, "I can handle a broken plate, Josh."

She rose and threw the pieces in the trash and finally glanced at Josh, who hadn't said a thing. "What?"

"You're beautiful when you're annoyed."

"Damn it, Gardner, cut that out. You keep promising to back off, and then here you are, giving me those goo-goo eyes again."

"Goo-goo eyes?"

"You know, the way your eyes go all dark and intense and I just know you're thinking about kissing me, and I don't want you to think about kissing me."

"Why are my thoughts a concern, Libby?"

"Because when you're thinking them, I can't help but think them, too, and kissing you isn't what I had in mind."

"Even if I promise that all I want from you is a kiss?"

"Josh," she warned.

"Even if I tell you that I keep promising myself I won't think about kissing you anymore, and then you get annoyed and turn all gorgeous in your righteous anger and all I can think of is kissing you until your mind goes numb and you forget why you're annoyed?"

"Josh," she warned again, softer this time.

"You don't want to kiss me, and I sure as hell don't want to want to kiss you, and yet, like I said before, there it is, that kiss just standing there between us, waiting to be had. Maybe if we just kiss, we'll go on with our night and not think about it anymore."

"I don't think that's much of a plan."

"To be honest, neither do I, but I don't have a better one. Just one small kiss, Libby."

"But—" She started to argue, but she was interrupted by his lips finding hers. Kissing Joshua Gardner was addictive. Libby just wanted to fill herself with him, tasting, touching, learning. There was so much to learn about this man.

Josh broke off the kiss and gave a small whistle of appreciation. "I think we need to clear the air."

Libby whirled around, turning her attention to taking the leftovers from the fridge and popping the lids off the containers. "I think you need to clear out of my kitchen," she muttered.

Lightly Josh rested his hand on her shoulder. "I like you, and I think you like me—"

"Some of the time."

"And I think we both enjoy kissing. Neither of us is looking for a long-term relationship, but maybe that's a good thing."

She dropped the lids in a pile and turned to face him. "A good thing?"

"We're both going into this with realistic expectations. We like each other. I don't think you can deny that if you're honest. So, let's stop this kiss-and-run nonsense. We're adults, Libby. Let's just agree up front that we're attracted to each other, and stop making such a big deal out of it."

"But what about Meg? She could get hurt—"

"Do you really think I'd do anything to hurt Meg? I like her. She's a bright, cute kid, and if I'd had a daughter, I'd want her to be just like Meg. We've played some video games together and I'm taking her to a party. That's it. She understands that. Why don't you?"

"But you might hurt her when you leave," Libby whispered, voicing her deepest fear. One man had already walked out on Meg, and Libby wasn't about to let another come into their…Meg's life and do it again.

"Libby, life is full of people coming and going, but I'm not going anywhere. I just opened my office, and I plan on staying. So even if you and I get over our kissing-fests, I'll still make time for Meg. That's one promise I have no trouble making."

Libby had more arguments, she was sure she did, but for the life of her she couldn't remember one. "I…" She started then stopped.

"Oh, hell," she muttered as she catapulted herself back into his arms and kissed the socks off him.

"Oh, hell is right," he muttered as they came up for air.

"Now that we've got that out of our system, let's eat some leftovers." She turned back to the leftovers and started loading them onto the table.

"Dinner. You've got it." Josh opened the silverware drawer and took out three sets.

"And, Josh?" Libby said quietly as she took a plate out of the cupboard to replace the one she'd broken.

"Hmm?"

"You hurt Meg—"

"You don't need any threats, Libby. I don't plan on hurting Meg." *Or hurting you,* he silently added.

He'd give her space, and allow her to adjust to the idea of— He mentally paused, not sure how to describe the relationship they'd just agreed to, but whatever it was, he would take his time exploring it.

He watched her bustle about the kitchen, and suppressed a grin. Libby McGuiness might be prickly on the outside, but she was soft and pliant in his arms. And though he hadn't lied—he wasn't looking for some lifetime commitment—Josh knew he did plan to find Libby back in his arms as soon as possible.

Chapter Seven

Libby managed to avoid Josh the rest of the weekend. Actually, avoiding him wasn't hard since he never called and didn't stop back over. She was relieved, she assured herself Sunday night as she went to bed.

And she was relieved, she assured herself Monday as she went to work. Relieved that she had gone two whole days without Joshua Gardner kissing her or messing with her life. But she faced up to the fact that it was Monday, and she was back to work, so she probably would *have* to see him. Not that she wanted to.

Nope. The fact she was going to have to see Joshua Gardner wasn't why she felt a hundred pounds lighter when she opened the shop Monday morning, bright and early. And she assured herself on Tuesday and

Wednesday she was relieved he wasn't pursuing her anymore. It was obvious that Joshua Gardner had got kissing her out of his system, and Libby was relieved.

Very relieved.

The weight that seemed to bear down upon her chest every now and again was just the stress of the holidays, nothing more.

When Thursday dawned bright and sunny with still no word from Josh, Libby was even *more* relieved. Of course, the two of them still had to finalize the party plans, but the worst was over and they still had plenty of time. No reason to bother him, she thought as her hand hovered near the telephone receiver. She snatched the offending appendage back from the phone and didn't dial the number she'd long since memorized.

Feeling disgusted, and momentarily in between customers, Libby bagged the garbage, twisting the tie on the bag with maybe a bit more force than required. She didn't give a hoot that Josh kissed her Friday and then ignored her for five days—five very long days.

She banged out the back door of the shop and stomped to the garbage bin. She pushed at the heavy door on top of the garbage bin, shivering in the bitter Erie wind.

"Here, let me help."

She turned and practically ran into Josh. "I've got it," she gritted out between her clenched teeth.

"What's the matter with you?" He crowded close,

sandwiching Libby between his body and the garbage bin.

She pushed at him, needing some space. Touching Josh didn't appeal to her at all, which is why those five long days of respite were so welcomed.

"What's the matter with me? What could be the matter with me? Nothing. That's what's wrong. I'm just throwing out the garbage and getting back to work."

He grinned. "You're mad I haven't called." He reached past her and opened the garbage bin.

"You're nuts," she scoffed, tossing the bag into the garbage bin. She turned, but Josh was still right behind her and she had nowhere to go but into his arms, and in Joshua Gardner's arms was the last place she wanted to be.

"Tomorrow night," he said softly, his voice a caress.

"Tomorrow night, what?" Libby asked, hating herself for the way her heart raced just because Josh was near.

"You and me on a date. No parties to plan, no little girls, no old ladies. Just you and me, and a movie." He reached out and pushed a stray strand of hair out of Libby's face.

She smacked at his hand. "A date? You don't call for five days—"

"You were counting?" Josh sounded pleased at the thought.

"It doesn't take much math to count to five, Gardner." She shoved against his chest, but Josh didn't budge.

"But if you were counting, it does mean you've been thinking about me."

"Don't flatter yourself."

Josh chuckled. "I doubt you'd let me."

When Libby started to protest, his finger against her lips was enough to silence her. Actually, his finger against her lips was enough to send her already-rapid heart rate skyrocketing.

"Now, about tomorrow," he said.

"I don't think a date would be wise." No, wise would be turning around and running from this man who had the ability to make her feel like an awkward teenager.

"I thought we agreed we could be adults, we could kiss and I think we could even manage dating without running to the altar. It's just a date, Libby." He crowded closer. "And I haven't called because I told you I'd give you space. Five days was all the space I could manage."

"And now you want a date?"

"I wanted a date five days ago, but waited until today to ask."

His hand toyed with her hair, weaving his fingers through it in a very distracting way. She pushed at his hand, but there was little force in the action. What on earth was wrong with her?

"Just a date—not a marriage," he said soothingly. "So don't start your running. Just two friendly people going out together."

"And kissing?" she asked, unsure if she wanted kissing as part of the agenda or not. Okay, she knew she wanted kissing, but she wasn't sure she wanted to want kissing.

"Oh, yeah, and kissing." His fingers left her hair and returned to her lips. He slowly, softly traced their outline.

"I need to think." Her voice was breathy and unfamiliar, just like the feelings Josh inspired were unfamiliar.

"I'll be at your place tomorrow at six. I'm betting Pearly, Josie or Mabel will agree to watch Meg."

"But—"

"I've been patient, Libby. Five days exhausted all of it though. Tomorrow at six." He turned and headed toward his office's back door. Gotta go," he called.

And he was gone.

Libby wandered back into the shop, wondering at the lightness that seemed to envelop her at the thought of seeing Josh tomorrow on a date. A real date.

Then the terror set in. A date? How long had it been since she'd gone on a real date?

"What's wrong with you, girl?" Pearly asked, pulling Libby from her reverie.

"He doesn't call me for five days, and then blithely

announces, when he corners me against the garbage bin, that he wants to date me.''

"I assume *he* is Josh. And I thought you were already dating.'' Pearly was loading towels into the small washer in the back room of the store.

"No, we've planned a party, done some shopping, had dinner at my place, been thrown together by friends and—''

"And kissing. You've done some kissing.'' Pearly scooped the detergent into the washer and slammed the lid before turning to Libby.

"Well, yes, there's that. But we weren't dating. Dating is something I say yes to. It's something I do on purpose without any conniving friends setting me up.''

"So what's the problem?'' Pearly lounged against the washer.

"I don't know what to do. I mean, I know I should say no. Josh and I…well, we've both agreed to keep it casual, but I'm still nervous.''

"I've watched you for years, Liberty Rae McGuiness. You hardly date, and when you do, you break it off before anything serious can develop. You run. Now here's a man who's working next door. He's hard to run from, and from the looks of it, if you do run he just might chase you. So, don't you go making up your mind that the two of you dating won't work before you give it a chance.''

Before Libby could find a retort to Pearly's armchair psychiatry, Pearly asked, "Did I ever tell you about my uncle Pernius?"

Libby could feel a smile touch her lips despite the tumultuous thoughts Josh inspired. "No, I don't believe you have."

"Well, Uncle Pern used to make decisions on the spot. You want this or that? Well he never stopped to think, he just up and said which one he was wantin'." As Pearly told her story, her Southern accent became decidedly thicker. "Well, one day the Widow Stella Horny—honest to goodness, that was her name—well, she up and said to Uncle Pern, 'You either marry me or do without.'

"Well, Uncle Pern wasn't overly fond of doing without—you remember I told you about my pa's insatiable appetites. Well they run in the family. So he says, 'Guess I'll be a marryin' you, then.'

"They did and his life was living hell for the next twenty-eight years, three months and four days—I know the number because he counted and used to tell everyone he met how long he suffered. Aunt Stella, it seems, didn't feel that she needed to satisfy his hungers once his ring was on her finger and his name attached to hers. So poor Uncle Pern suffered and, by the time Aunt Stella had gone to her final release, Uncle Pern found he couldn't…well, couldn't raise the flag anymore, much to his everlasting disappointment."

She paused, staring at Libby a moment, then asked, "Now, do you know what I'm trying to tell you?"

Libby laughed. "Never marry a woman named Horny because she might not be anymore when her name's been changed?"

"No," Pearly said, suddenly all seriousness. "You run from relationships, and it looks to me as if you're working up for a good fast sprint. I'm saying, don't make any decisions without really thinking them through, or you might find yourself regretting them for the next twenty-eight years, three months and four days."

"Twenty-eight years, three months and four days," Libby muttered as she sat in the passenger seat of Joshua's truck the following night.

He glanced at her. "Pardon?"

"To answer your question, I'm only out on this date so I don't regret not being here twenty-eight years, three months and four days from now."

Josh glanced her way. "Twenty-eight years, three months and three—"

"Four days."

"Four days," he amended. "So you think you would have regretted it if you'd said no to our date?"

"I don't know," Libby said with a sigh. She sank farther back in the seat and then admitted, "I guess it hasn't been going all that bad."

"You liked the movie?"

"More than you say you did." She chuckled, despite her nervousness. At the movie she'd forgotten she was on a date and simply enjoyed Josh's reactions.

He'd seemed more than slightly uncomfortable with the tears that flowed openly on and off the screen for a large percentage of the two hours and ten minutes they'd spent at the movie.

"It wasn't that bad. And I should get some credit with you for being a gentleman and letting you pick that chick-flick."

"Chick-flick?" She laughed. "I noticed you were a little teary-eyed when the credits rolled."

"Real men don't cry at chick-flicks." He paused and grinned. "Do you know why real men agree to go to those movies with their dates?"

"Why?" she asked, though she was sure he would have told her even if she hadn't asked.

"In the hopes that the girl *will* cry…all over his shoulder."

For a moment some of Libby's ease disappeared as an image of Mitch standing, listening to the doctor tell them that Meg was deaf, came into focus. She'd stood by his side, tears running down her face, more alone at that moment than she'd ever been.

Mitch hadn't offered her his shoulder, nor was he willing to cry on hers, or even lean on her. They'd stood there, two people whose lives were parallel, but separate. It was that separation that finally brought about the end of their marriage.

"I can't imagine any man wanting to be cried on," she said softly.

They drove in silence for a few minutes, before Josh turned onto her street. He pulled into Libby's driveway.

"Want to talk about it?" he asked.

There was concern in Josh's voice, and for a moment Libby wondered if he would have stood at her side and let her cry by herself, or if he would have reached out and held her, supporting her and letting her support him?

Needing to keep things light, she forced a laugh that sounded hollow to her ears. "Watch it, Gardner. First I catch you sniffling at a chick-flick, and now you're almost being tender. Either of those characteristics could destroy my manly-man image of you."

Willing to take his cue from her, Josh's voice lightened. "Libby, it's not the crying that turns men on, it's the opportunity to soothe a woman's fragile feelings."

"And just how would a real man do that?" she asked softly.

"Like this." He slid across the truck's bench seat, and hesitated a moment before wrapping his arms around her.

Libby knew she should pull away, but being held by Josh felt good. It felt right. And when his lips met hers, that feeling of rightness intensified, and grew until it was too much to bear. Libby pulled back, thankful

that Josh didn't push. If he had, she didn't know if
she could have pulled away a second time.

"I guess there's a lot I don't know about real men,"
she said with as much flippancy as she could muster.

"I guess you don't," he agreed. "I'd be happy to
teach you."

"That's what I'm afraid of."

Josh paused and studied her a moment. "Nope,
that's not fear I see in your eyes." *At least not this
time,* he thought.

"What do you see?"

"Eagerness." He paused again and searched those
beautiful blue eyes. Josh had looked into countless
eyes in the life of his practice, but he'd never seen
any that touched him the way Libby's did. "Yep, definitely eagerness."

"Have I ever mentioned you're arrogant?" There
was no heat in her voice.

"Maybe once or twice." He didn't try to kiss her
again. He was just content to hold her in his arms.

"Well, let me say it again. You're a very arrogant
man, Dr. Gardner."

"Arrogant and eager, too."

Libby laughed.

The sound sent Josh's heart racing. This is what
he'd been waiting for. Gone was the fearful watchful-
ness. Tonight he was experiencing the real Libby
McGuiness. Laughing, smart-mouthed and a heck of
a kisser.

Giving her five days of breathing room had been a good idea, though it had almost killed him. But it had been worth it. Libby had lost that hunted, wary look.

"Hey, Libby?"

"What now?" she asked with mock exasperation.

"How long has it been since you've parked like this?" Deliberately he let his hand drift lower down her back until it was resting on her waist.

"I park in this driveway every day," she said primly.

"I wasn't thinking about that kind of parking. I was thinking more along the lines of *Parking,* with a capital *P.* You know, sitting out here in this car and sucking face with abandon."

"I've already kissed you good night." Her arms still entwined around him, she gave a little squeeze.

"No. That was just an appetizer," Josh assured her.

"Why, Dr. Gardner, are you trying to compromise my virtue?" she said with a horrible attempt to mimic Pearly's Southern accent.

"I'm doing my darnedest, Ms. McGuiness. I'm doing my darnedest."

His lips found hers again, and again Josh experienced a sense of rightness, as if this woman had been made for his arms, her lips made for his lips. Gently he eased those lips apart and deepened the kiss, as his hand drifted lower down her back.

Libby melted into him, her arms clutching him

close, closer—meeting his kiss with a hunger that surprised as much as it delighted him.

Slowly she pulled back, and though everything in him demanded he hold on, Josh allowed her to move away.

"I have to go in," she said breathlessly.

"You have a curfew?" he teased.

"No, I have a daughter." Breathlessness and laughter were gone from her voice. Flat and final, Libby McGuiness was once again setting boundaries.

"I didn't forget about Meg, Libby," Josh said gently. He removed his arms and slid back to his side of the car, giving her distance.

She sighed. "I know. I just—"

"Needed to reestablish some boundaries. I know."

"You think you know me so well." Prickly, snippy Libby McGuiness was back, her wall once again firmly in place.

"Here, see if I've got this right. When Meg's father left, you closed off a whole piece of Libby McGuiness and decided to concentrate your energies on your daughter and your business. That's all well and good, Libby. You've done a fantastic job with both, but you're still an individual with needs of her own— needs that are separate from both the business and Meg."

"And you're volunteering to help me with that side of myself—with my needs?" Bristly and snippy.

Josh tamped down a spurt of irritation. How long

would he have to spar with this woman? How many times would he have to prove himself to her?

An even bigger question was, why was he bothering? He kept telling himself that he wasn't looking for a relationship, and yet that was exactly what he was trying to establish with prickly Libby McGuiness.

Forcing himself to put on a calm facade, Josh answered, "I think I already have. I think for the first time in a long time you're remembering you're not just a business owner and a mom. I think tonight you remembered that you're a woman with needs that are totally separate from your business or your daughter."

"Arrogant as ever, Dr. Gardner. For your information, I've never forgotten I'm a woman." Even in the dim light the street lamp cast in the car, Josh could see Libby sit a bit straighter in the seat.

"Really? Other than myself, when's the last time you've been kissed by a man? Better yet, when's the last time you kissed a man?" The thought of Libby kissing anyone else gave Josh a burning feeling in the pit of his stomach.

"I…" Her voice trailed off.

"Ha. You don't know."

"I do, too. I just don't kiss and tell," she said, all prim and proper.

But not too proper, he knew. No, the bristles and properness disappeared when she was in his arms. "Oh, shut up, Libby, and kiss me."

"You are the most frustrating man I've ever met."

But even as she said the words, she slid across the seat and back into his arms.

"And you are the most kissable woman, despite your inability to park a car and the prickly facade you like to maintain."

"Oh, just kiss me," she muttered.

"What about Meg?" he mumbled as he planted a tiny row of kisses up her neck and across her jawline.

"She'll be fine for a few more minutes."

Half an hour later Libby crept into the house.

"So, how was it?" Pearly asked.

"The movie was fine, though I'm not sure Josh would say the same."

"Not the movie. The parking."

"I don't know what you mean." She leaned down and unlaced her boots, unwilling to look Pearly in the eye, sure that her guilt was written boldly on her face. Well, not exactly guilt. No, guilt wasn't what she was feeling about Josh, but she couldn't quite pin a name on the feelings he inspired.

"I don't know what you mean," she repeated, rising and unbuttoning her coat.

"Sure you do. You two were out in the car for almost three quarters of an hour. Are you going to try and tell me that all you were doing was talking? Not that talking's bad. Why, getting to know each other is important to a relationship, but I have a feeling that you were getting to know each other with more than words."

"Pearly!" Her fingers stilled on the last button.

"And, of course, the fact that the windows got all foggy meant I couldn't see much, but did lead me to believe that you were doing more than talking."

"I don't know why you all seem bound and determined to push Josh and me together." She forced herself to finish removing her coat, forced herself to try and sound calm. "Why, he's an arrogant, opinionated man—"

"*Man* is the operative word, sweetums. All men are arrogant and opinionated, but not all of them can kiss a girl senseless, and by the look on your face, I'm guessing that's exactly what Joshua did."

"So you're saying I'm senseless?" She bristled.

"You can't pick a fight with me, Libby, hon. And I'm not saying you're senseless. Actually, if you had a little less sense and worried a little less, it might be better. What I was saying is that while you're kissing Joshua, you forget."

"Forget what?" She didn't really need to ask, she already knew. When she kissed Josh she forgot everything.

"Forget all your absurd reasons for avoiding relationships."

"I don't avoid—" she started to say, then cut off the lie. "My reasons for avoiding relationships aren't absurd."

"Libby, honey, you've made avoiding emotional connections an art. Do you know how many years it took for you to open up to Josie and me? And we work with you every day, and yet you maintained that safe distance. You'd probably still be keeping us outside of your boundaries if we hadn't hammered away at that wall. You might not have noticed it, but Josie and I can be persistent.''

Libby snorted. ''I think that might be one of the biggest understatements ever.''

''But despite the fact you've let us in, there's still a section of yourself that you keep behind that wall. You think it makes you safe, but it just makes you lonely.''

Pearly's words hit a little too close to what Josh had said. ''Do you really feel as if I'm trying to keep myself separate?''

''Honey chil'.'' Libby could sense some down-home wisdom was about to be imparted by the thickening of Pearly's accent. ''My mama always said that a woman afraid to love was a woman afraid to live. And, sweetums, you're about as afraid as they come.''

''I'm not afraid, I'm—'' Libby searched for a word ''—cautious. I'm just cautious.''

''That's what you tell yourself.'' Pearly shook her head. ''Now, Meggie's asleep and I'm leaving before I get myself fired.''

''Like you'd listen if I fired you. No one listens to me. I tell Mabel I don't want to chair this stupid party, and here I am chairing it. I tell all of you to stop trying to throw Josh and me together, and you're still throwing. I tell Josh I'm not kissing him—I tell myself I'm not kissing him—''

"And there you are, sitting in the car parking with him?"

"Yeah," Libby admitted with a sigh. "So, I don't imagine if I told you that you were fired you'd stay fired."

"Well, there is that, but I'm not taking any chances." She put on her coat and opened the door. "You think about what I said."

"The only thing I'm thinking about is going to bed."

Pearly tsked once or twice but left without making any more noise.

That was good. That was great. Libby was tired of people telling her she was running away from life. She was tired of being told a woman had to have a man to be fulfilled.

She was more than filled—filled to the point of overflow. She had her job, a business she owned. She had friends. Oh, those friends might occasionally be pains in her butt, but they were good and Libby knew she could always count on them. And last, but not least—first, as a matter of fact—she had Meg. Her daughter was the best part of her life.

Why on earth did she need a man to clutter things up? He would certainly complicate things. And Libby didn't need any more complications.

She walked down the hall and couldn't resist opening Meg's door. Her daughter was a wild sleeper. Her hair fanned over the pillow, the covers twisted into knots, and…she was utterly the most wonderful thing Libby had ever accomplished in her life.

Libby couldn't resist straightening the covers a bit.

"You're home," Meg signed sleepily. The hall light peeking through the door illuminated what she said.

"I'm home and you're supposed to be asleep," she scolded her daughter. It was a relief being the one in charge, the one doing the scolding for a change.

"I was, but you woke me up."

Libby leaned down and kissed Meg's forehead. "Sorry."

Meg sat up in bed. "How was it?"

Libby sensed there would be no quick escape, and sat on the edge of the bed, resigned to a late-night discussion with a ten-year-old. Though she knew what Meg was asking, Libby couldn't help but hope she could avoid the discussion.

She played dumb and asked, "How was what?"

"Josh," Meg fingerspelled.

"We had a nice time." *Nice.* Nice might be the appropriate word to describe any number of things, but it seemed inadequate to describe her evening with Josh. Her thoughts turned momentarily to their Parking with a capital *P* in the driveway.

No, *nice* wasn't the word she'd use to describe her evening with Josh, but Meg didn't need to know just how much more than *nice* the evening was.

"I'm glad," Meg said.

"Why?"

"I like Josh and he likes me. He likes you, too." And that, to a ten-year-old's way of thinking, was enough.

For someone who'd been against her dating Josh, Meg had done a total turnaround. What was it about this man that charmed women old enough to be his grandmother, and young enough to be his daughter?

Libby tucked the covers in around Meg, determined to put an end to this discussion, but instead of getting up and leaving Meg so the poor kid could get some sleep, she found herself saying, "But when you thought that first business meeting was a date, you were mad."

"I was wrong. You're happy with Josh, happier than you've been in a long time. I hope he sticks around."

But he wouldn't stick around, Libby knew. He might like them both, but eventually he'd leave just like everyone else did.

Like Mitch had.

Pearly had hit the nail on the head with her armchair psychoanalysis—Libby ran from relationships. She remembered when she'd first met Mitch. The feelings she'd had for him were so big, so grand that she would never believe they could wither up and die. And yet they had. If what she had felt for Mitch—the man she'd been married to for four years, the man she'd had a child with—couldn't last, what could?

Nothing. These feelings she had for Josh were transitory. Lust. That's all. The feelings would eventually fade away.

What she felt for Meg was timeless and endless. She gave her another small kiss on the forehead and slipped from the room, stopping to steal one more glance at her daughter just before she shut the door. Meg's eyes were closed, and it appeared she was already back to sleep.

Looking at Meg, talking to Meg, marveling at the wonder of this child she'd raised, that was what mattered. Meg was all that mattered.

How was Libby's relationship with Josh—a relationship she hadn't even begun to define—going to affect her daughter? When he left, and he would leave, would Meg be hurt? And did that potential for being hurt outweigh what Josh had to offer Meg here and now?

Libby didn't know.

All she did know was that being with Josh made her feel alive, and she wasn't ready to let go of that feeling. Maybe she and Meg could grab enough happy memories to dull the ache of losing Josh when it came.

Slowly she changed into her pajamas and crawled into her big, lonely bed, replaying the evening in her mind. Thoughts of Josh and his sense of humor, his seemingly genuine fondness for her daughter, and his kisses—definitely his kisses. That's what circled through her mind as she tried to sleep, not the questions she couldn't answer.

And when sleep finally did claim her, those thoughts haunted her dreams, as well…. Hot, erotic dreams.

Chapter Eight

"So?" Libby asked that weekend, though she really didn't need to hear how the party at Mercyhurst had gone. The answer was written all over Meg's face.

She'd spent the afternoon of the Mercyhurst Sign Language party waiting and worrying. She worried they wouldn't have a good time, she worried they'd have too good a time. She worried Josh would feel out of place, she worried Josh would feel too much at home. She… Well, after this afternoon, Libby had decided she had made worrying an art form.

But from the expressions on Josh and Meg's faces, all her worry had been for nothing. Meg was practically glowing.

And so was Josh—glowing in a grown-up male sort of way.

Darn. Wherever Libby turned, there he was. Haunting her days...and her nights. And she knew she was going to remember that he looked as excited as Meg at this particular moment in time.

Trying to sign while she removed her jacket, Meg practically tied herself in knots but managed to say, "Josh learned to sing 'Jingle Bells' with me. Tell him to show you."

"Meg wants you to show me how the two of you sign 'Jingle Bells,'" Libby dutifully repeated.

Josh removed his jacket and put it in the closet. "Did she mention how bad I am?"

Libby laughed. "No, I don't think she did."

"Tell her thanks."

Meg laughed as Libby signed Josh's statement to her. "He's not bad." She paused and added, "Not too bad. He does the jingle part really good."

Libby grinned. The jingle bell part of the song required pretty much just a shaking of the hands.

"Are you ready?" Meg asked Josh, and Libby translated.

They led her into the living room. She'd lit a fire in the fireplace earlier, and it was warm and inviting. Libby curled on the couch as she watched Josh and her daughter laughing their way through the signed version of "Jingle Bells." Meg had been very generous. Josh was horrible. But it was the sheer awkwardness of his attempts that was so...well, endearingly cute.

When Meg picked up the tempo, leaving Josh in the dust, he leaned over and slugged her shoulder, ever so casually. That one small gesture said so much.

Josh saw a little girl when he looked at Meg—nothing more, nothing less. And though she kept smiling, Libby felt her throat constrict. When the song finished, and Meg and Josh took their bows, that constriction threatened to outgrow her ability to hide it.

Joshua Gardner had told her once that most people thought he was nice. And though Libby had avoided admitting it to him, those people were right. Libby eyed the dark-haired man who was laughing with her daughter. Those people he'd referred to didn't know the half of it; Josh was a very nice man.

"I'm going to go see if Jackie or anyone's online, okay?" Meg asked, and then took off without waiting for an answer.

Libby watched her run down the hall, and wanted to call her back. She wanted to chase after her daughter and continue to use the ten-year-old as a buffer between her and Josh. With Meg in the room it was easier to relax around Josh and concentrate on things other than kissing. But as soon as Meg left, Libby couldn't help but glance at Josh's very kissable lips.

Darn. She had to stop this nonsense.

Libby had been unloading the dishwasher when they'd come in and she decided to finish doing so, anything to keep her hands busy and off Josh.

He rose and helped, silently matching her movements and generally getting in her way.

He was in her way a lot. At her side, in her thoughts. In her fantasies. Why couldn't she seem to shake this man?

"You know, we seem to end up in here a lot." He stacked the plates and deposited them on the counter.

"What?" Libby nervously began to rinse the dirty breakfast dishes.

"Here in the kitchen, doing dishes and…"

"And?" She shut off the water, then turned and bumped into Josh.

"And kissing." His voice was low and husky. He advanced a step.

Libby tried to dodge his advance, but was stymied by the counter. "Josh," she warned.

"The dishwasher's empty." He reached out and gently brushed his hand against her cheek.

Libby resisted the urge to lean into the small caress, just as she was resisting the urge to plant her lips on his. Kissing Joshua Gardner was addictive.

Dishes, not kisses. Now that was a much safer topic to concentrate on than kissing.

"But there are still dishes to go into the dishwasher," she said weakly.

"They'll wait a minute. I've been thinking that after each part of the job is done we should kiss."

"Why?"

He closed what little space remained between them.

"Why kiss? Because it will make the next job go faster."

"How will our kissing make the next job go faster?" She should move, should slip past him and finish the job at hand. Better yet, Libby should show Josh to the door and get him out of her house and out of her head.

Trouble was, getting Josh out of her house might be easier than getting him out of her head. Thoughts of him interrupted her days, and her nights.

"If we kiss after each job, we'll be so anxious to get another kiss, we'll rush right through it, so kissing will make the work go faster."

She was sandwiched between the counter and Josh. The warmth of his body was comforting somehow.

"That's your great idea?" she asked.

"Do you have a better one?"

"How about this?" No longer willing to let Josh take the lead, and disregarding all her misgivings about getting involved with him, Libby moved into his arms and kissed him. Just this once she allowed herself to taste the wonder of him with abandon. She feasted on his lips, deepening the kiss and losing herself in his taste.

So long.

It had been so long since she'd felt this kind of desire, this sense of rightness. Finally breathless, she pulled away, awed by her daring.

Josh's breath brushed her sensitive lips. "It seems to me that was my idea."

"Pardon?" Libby forgot whatever they'd been talking about the second her lips touched his.

"You said you had a better idea, but it was my idea to kiss after each job," he maintained.

"No, yours was to kiss after each job. Mine was to kiss whenever we could."

He reached out and traced her lips lightly with his finger. "I'm glad."

"Glad we kissed?" She squeezed past him, needing some distance. Being close to Josh was overwhelming. She attacked the dishes with gusto. Squirting some soap in the sink and rinsing them before loading the old dishwasher, which needed the added help in cleaning the dishes. Why she bothered running them through the dishwasher, she wasn't sure.

Just like she wasn't sure why she was here, in the kitchen, playing with fire.

"Glad we kissed—" he took a plate and put it into the dishwasher for her "—and glad we're here, together, not fighting, just doing dishes together. In case I haven't mentioned it before, I really like your kitchen. And I can't tell you how much I enjoyed today."

"A party with a bunch of grade school kids, or are you talking about the kissing?" Libby handed him a glass.

Josh accepted the glass and loaded it, falling into

the rhythm of working with Libby. "Now, don't get me wrong, kissing you is addictive. But the rest of it—being with you, being with Meg. I enjoy it. It feels right."

Right for now, Libby was sure, though she didn't say it. She didn't want to start another argument with Josh. As a matter of fact, if she was honest, she didn't really want to talk at all, because talking made her worry about how much it would hurt when Josh was gone.

No. She didn't want to talk and most especially didn't want to think rationally. She just wanted to kiss him. When she was kissing Josh she could forget the little voice that kept whispering that she was going to be hurt when he left.

Hands soapy from the dishes, she turned, wrapped her arms around a very surprised Josh and kissed him again. Soft and playful, she pecked his lips and then flicked some bubbles at him.

"Hey!" He laughed as he wiped the bubbles from his nose. "What was that for? We haven't finished loading the dishwasher yet, so the kiss was unscheduled, and the bubbles were uncalled for."

"I don't like being predictable—"

"You don't have to worry about that," he teased.

"—so I don't want to kiss you on a schedule."

"Oh." He scooped up a handful of suds and plopped them on her head. "I'm not predictable, either. But I liked my kissing schedule."

"I liked the kissing part." She wiped the suds off her head and placed her desudded hands on his shoulder. "I like the kissing part a whole bunch."

"Who am I to argue with a lady?" The laughter quickly gave way to more kissing.

Libby knew she should be worried, but while she was in his arms, while she was kissing him, she could think of nothing but Josh, and at that moment, it was enough.

A stomp brought Libby back to her senses. She pushed against Josh, separating them, but not soon enough to save her daughter from getting an eyeful of their embrace.

Meg stood in the doorway, eyeing the adults. "Having fun?" she asked.

Libby could feel the heat rise to her cheeks. "I...I had something in my eye and Josh was helping me get it out."

"It looked more like kissing to me," Meg said slyly.

"Meg!"

"Well, he was. And you were kissing him back." The precocious child had the nerve to laugh. "Relax. I like Josh, remember? I just came to see if he wanted to play some video games, but I think he'd rather stay here with you."

With that, Meg scampered back toward her room.

"You know, that's one of the few times you haven't interpreted automatically for me," Josh said softly.

Libby startled. She'd forgotten him for a moment. She whirled around. "Now look what you've done."

"What I've done?" The infuriating man had the gall to laugh. "Seems to me you were there kissing, too."

"I...well, I shouldn't..." Libby resisted the urge to stomp her foot in frustration. Men and daughters—she couldn't decide which was more frustrating.

"I should have known better," she said with all the decisiveness she could muster.

"Libby, we were just kissing, nothing more. I don't think witnessing it will cause Meg any serious long-term psychological damage. She didn't seem upset."

Libby didn't want to listen to some ophthalmologist try his hand at psychoanalyzing her daughter. She didn't want to talk about kissing, about not kissing, about anything. So instead of talking, she turned back to the dishes.

"So now you're going to give me the silent treatment?"

"Maybe. Maybe *not* talking to you is a good idea."

"Was she upset, Libby?" He took a plate and loaded it into the dishwasher, his hand extended waiting for the next. "I've learned a thing or two about body language watching Meg, and she didn't seem upset. You seemed upset, but not Meg."

Libby ignored him and just kept washing.

"Was she upset, Libby?"

"No. No she wasn't." She glared at Josh.

"So why are you?" His voice was a soft caress—seductive and tempting.

"I…" Libby desperately tried to remember why she was upset. All she could think of was how utterly kissable his lips looked, and how inviting his arms seemed.

"I think I'm losing my mind," she lamented as she walked into that very tempting embrace.

"That's only right because I've already lost mine," Josh said just before his lips, those lusciously kissable lips, claimed hers.

"You've lost it," Josh said in the middle of Libby's paper-strewn spare room. They'd spent a quiet afternoon wrapping the gifts they'd bought for the party. Meg was off with Josie, leaving Libby and Josh to finish up the party preparations.

"There's nothing left to do," he said.

"But we've—"

"Libby, it's all done." He balled a scrap of paper and shot it at the clear recycling bag.

"What if we forgot—?"

"We didn't forget anything," he soothed. "And so what if we did? It's a party for the PSBA, not for the president and visiting dignitaries. We've got a hall, food and gifts…. Anything else we've forgotten can't be all that important."

Libby crinkled her brow. "I just want it to be perfect."

Josh reached out and ran a finger lightly across her forehead. "Perfection is sorely overrated. And right now we're going to be a lot less than perfect.... We're going to play hooky."

He watched Libby survey the mess they'd made wrapping presents for Santa to hand out. "We really should clean up."

"We'll clean up later. We've got—" Josh glanced at his watch "—two hours until Josie brings Meg back and we're going to have some fun."

Josh didn't mind planning the party with Libby because it gave him an excuse to be with her. But suddenly he wanted more—he wanted to get away from her house, from the party. He wanted her all to himself. He wanted to be the sole focus of her attention.

"What do you have in mind?" Libby asked, suspicion tingeing her tone.

He chuckled. "Get your mind out of the gutter, McGuiness. Maybe it's time we tried something other than sparring with each other, planning this party or necking."

"I like necking," she protested.

"I actually like all three, but let's try something new." He stood and reached out a hand. As always, a tiny jolt of *something* accompanied her touch as he pulled her to her feet.

"What?" she asked, trailing after him as he left the room.

"Put on something warm and trust me." Josh

searched his childhood memories of Erie for someplace to take her, someplace away from everything and everyone.

Presque Isle. In the summer the sliver of land that shot out into Lake Erie was crowded, one of Erie County's major tourist attractions, but Josh remembered its beauty didn't dim in the winter. And the wide expanse of beach covered in its winter coat of snow and ice was breathtaking.

"Where are we going?" she asked as he backed the truck out of her driveway.

"Trust me," he said again.

They rode in companionable silence across town. Libby couldn't help sneaking an occasional glance at the man driving the huge truck. Why was she here when every sensible part of her mind was screaming that time she spent with this man was dangerous?

Libby wasn't sure. All she knew was that whenever she was with him she felt…alive. They made their way across town and down Peninsula Drive. Libby purposely looked out the windows; staring at Josh was disconcerting. She wasn't sure what to feel, what to expect. Watching Waldameer Park, and the old Peninsula Drive-in out the window was easier than watching Josh and trying to pin a name on the emotions he evoked.

"We're here," he said, pulling the truck into a parking space on Beach Three.

"You're way too close to that car," Libby said.

Josh had pulled the oversize truck into a parallel spot and was practically sitting on the blue Tracker in front of them. "You've got tons of room—that's the only other car here—and still you're right on his bumper."

"He's got plenty of room to pull forward."

Libby simply raised an eyebrow.

Josh slipped the truck into Reverse and backed off a couple feet. "Happy?"

"I'm sure the Tracker's driver will be. You and Meg might make fun of my distance from the curb when I park, but you are a bumper hugger."

"You dare impugn my driving ability?" he growled.

"More than dare. I'll scream it from the rooftops. Dr. Joshua Gardner is a bumper-climbing, parking-space hog."

"You know what this means?" he asked.

"What?"

"War."

With a shriek, Libby burst from the truck and dashed across the snow-covered beach with Josh right on her heels. She glanced behind her to see where he was, and that was all the opening Josh needed. He tackled her, pinning her beneath him.

"Why, Dr. Gardner, what do you think you're going to do now?" she asked in a Pearly-esque Southern belle accent.

"I think you'd better brace yourself. There's only

one thing to do with women who impugn my driving—''

''Not your driving, your parking abilities,'' she corrected.

''My parking abilities. I'm afraid I'm going to have to kiss you.''

''Oh, no. Say it isn't so. That would be torture, pure and simple. And one slight disparagement of your parking abilities shouldn't force me to suffer so.'' Her mittened fingers dug at the snow and formed a haphazard snowball.

''Oh, I could think of even worse *tortures* for you, but since this is a public place, we'll settle for a simple kiss.''

Libby watched Josh's lips begin their descent. ''Um, Josh?'' she said.

''Hmm?''

''You can't park.'' She plopped the snowball in his face, and as he sputtered and wiped snow from his face, she rolled and pushed her way out from under him, tossing him into the snow as she made her escape, sprinting across the deserted beach.

Josh was on her heels in a moment. ''Caught ya,'' he said, snagging her by the shoulders and spinning her to face him. ''Now what should I do with you?''

''How about just hold me?'' she asked softly.

''Hmm. Good idea. If I'm holding you it will be harder for you to attack.'' He pulled her into his arms, her back to his chest, and simply held her.

They stood, watching the late-afternoon sun sink behind the ice dunes. "I love it out here in the summer, but I'll confess I've never been out here in the winter. That was a mistake," Libby said, her voice a soft whisper that was almost too loud for the winter-quiet beach.

"I haven't been here since I was a kid, but it's still the same, still one of the most beautiful places on earth." He looked at the woman who fit so neatly in his arms. "And being here with you makes it even more beautiful." He placed a chaste kiss on her neck.

Libby searched for something to say, but couldn't find the words. Instead she simply snuggled more securely into his embrace. Aggravation, annoyance, laughter, companionship and silence. She'd found them all with this man. And for a moment, she pushed aside her fears and just let herself revel in the quiet rightness of the moment.

And for the moment, that was enough.

Chapter Nine

It wasn't until the last child sat on Santa's lap and received his present that Libby breathed a sigh of relief. Santa was leaving, the presents had all been handed out and people were helping themselves to the brunch.

Josh had been right; they hadn't forgotten anything. The Christmas party was over and had been a great success. Now her job with Josh was done.

Thank goodness.

She was relieved, she assured herself. Oh, she'd still see him, at least for a while. Neither of them had gotten kissing out of their systems quite yet. But eventually they would, and then they'd gradually see less and less of each other until finally they were just neighbors, just members of the Perry Square Business Association.

"Libby?"

Libby realized that Mabel was at the microphone on St. Gert's auditorium stage and was saying her name.

"Libby? Yoo-hoo."

Libby gave a little wave back, feeling a hint of warmth creep into her cheeks. Everyone was looking at her.

Josh sidled up at her elbow. "She wants us on the stage, and I don't think she's going to let us off the hook. Mabel is persistent."

Persistent? No, Mabel was a pain in the butt. "What does she want?"

"How do I know?" Josh whispered, leading her toward the stage.

"Josh and Libby, on behalf of the Perry Square Business Association, I just want to thank you for the marvelous afternoon."

Applause filled St. Gert's hall.

"We wanted to do something special for you in appreciation." Mabel beckoned at someone offstage. Pearly and Josie—her hair an extrabrilliant shade of red in honor of the holiday—came across the stage.

Libby felt an acute pang of panic. The three of them looked way too pleased. "I don't like the looks of this," Libby muttered to Josh.

Josie and Pearly handed Libby a piece of paper.

Mabel said, "The PSBA has arranged for a night out on the town for the two of you. A night to just kick back and relax after all the work you've done on the party. Leo's Limos has donated a limo for an evening out on the town. And Waves has donated a five-star dinner. So the only worry you'll have is picking the date to go. It's not much of a thanks, but we wanted to do something to let you both know how much we appreciate all your hard work on our behalf.''

Everyone applauded and there was nothing that Libby could do but smile and thank the terrible match-making trio. She could see through them. Everyone in the room could see through them and this blatant attempt to make sure she and Josh still saw each other now that their *job* was over.

"And we're baby-sitting Meg, as well," Pearly whispered. "So you've got no excuses."

No excuses maybe, but someday soon Libby was going to have her revenge. All three were single ladies and what was good for the stylist was good for the employees and the acupuncturist. Oh, yes, she would have revenge, and it would be glorious.

Josh stepped up to the microphone. "Thanks, everyone. I'm sure Libby and I will enjoy ourselves. And I'd like to thank you all for making me feel like I'm a part of the community. I hope to be a part of the PSBA for years to come."

"You two work well together," Mabel said to Libby as they walked off the stage.

"Yes, but now it's over, except for the cleaning up."

"Pearly, Josie and I are taking Meg to the mall, then dropping her off at the Hendersons, remember?" Mabel said.

"After we're done cleaning up, right?"

"Now, Libby, we'd stay and help, but you know how the holiday crowds can be at the mall. We want to get up there and get started, or we'll never finish before they close. You know how long Meg takes to deliberate over everything. It's even worse when it's your present. Last year we must have gone into every store, and then returned to half of them before she made up her mind."

"You're going to leave me to clean up all by myself?"

Mabel had said she was good at delegating and it was obvious she was.

"Josh will stay." Mabel's grin held no apology for her blatant manipulation.

Of course. This was just another way to throw her together with Josh. Well, this time Libby could take it. After today the matchmaking trio would no longer have the party as an excuse to get the two of them together. Neither would Josh.

Neither would she.

She'd miss him, she admitted to herself—and only to herself. She'd miss him and his kisses.

"Fine." She shooed at Mabel. "Just take Pearly, Josie and Meg and go. Just leave all the work to me."

"And Josh," Mabel reminded her.

"And Josh what?" Josh asked, joining them.

"Mabel, Josie and Pearly are taking Meg shopping and leaving the two of us to clean up."

"No problem. I think it looks worse than it is."

Libby glanced around the room and snorted. Oh, it was worse all right, and she wasn't referring to the mess the PSBA had made of St. Gert's. Her emotions were even more of a mess. She was giddy one moment, annoyed the next and frightened out of her socks the next.

"You four just go on and have fun," Josh said. "Libby and I have it all under control here."

They spent the next hour picking up wrapping paper and sweeping the floor.

"I never understood wrapping presents," Libby said while tying off the umpteenth garbage bag. "All you end up doing is throwing all that paper away. I think it's just the paper industry's conspiracy, a way to sell more paper."

"Personally I've always been all for shopping bags." Josh finished tying his bag off and tossed it on the pile.

"Me, too."

"Another similarity," he said triumphantly, as if he'd been keeping a list. "Have you noticed just how many things we seem to have in common?"

"No." Libby pushed a cart of folding chairs toward the wall and out of the way.

"We both drink our coffee black." Josh slid another cart of folding tables next to the wall.

"So does half the country." She wiped her hands on the seat of her slacks. "I think we're about done."

"We both like old movies, too." Josh had obviously been giving their similarities a lot of thought.

They'd watched *Miracle on 34th Street* the night before and again he'd looked suspiciously close to tears when Natalie Woods got her house.

That Josh was a closet sad-movie-crier was an endearing secret, one that Libby enjoyed. Watching him discreetly sniffle his way through a film was almost as much fun as watching the movie.

"That's a classic. Everyone likes it," she protested. Too bad there was no real Santa, someone who could make dreams come true.

If there was a real Santa, what would she wish for? Would she wish for Josh, for the happily-ever-after that she used to believe could really happen? Libby shook her head. No, she didn't believe in Santa, or in dreams come true. Libby might believe in a happy-for-a-moment, but had learned the hard way that happily-ever-afters only happened in fairy tales.

"Oh, no. Not everyone likes classics," Josh assured her.

"Classics and coffee. That's two very broad likes. You'll have to do better than that."

"We both like Meg."

Libby finally grinned, allowing herself to be pulled

into the game. "Of course we both like Meg. How could anyone not like Meg? She's extraordinary."

Josh closed the distance that separated them. "Okay," he said huskily, "how about we both like kissing each other?"

"Now, that is a similar like that's out of the ordinary. It's also something I shouldn't like."

"But you do." Arrogant and confident, Josh slipped his hand around her, drawing her close.

Libby didn't pull back, but welcomed the embrace. If anyone had told her even last week that she'd learn to like kissing Josh, more than like, that she'd learn to anticipate the opportunities, she'd have called them nuts.

Maybe she was the one who was nuts, but if kissing Josh meant admitting to a little mental instability, then she'd gladly do it.

"You're awfully sure of yourself, Dr. Gardner," she said primly, even as she wrapped her arms around him.

"*Arrogant* is the word you like to use, Ms. McGuiness."

"Well, I guess when it comes to kissing you can afford to be a little arrogant," she admitted.

"Meaning?"

"Meaning when someone has reached the absolute height of any skill, they get to be a bit smug about it." She stood on tiptoe and brushed a series of light kisses along his jawline.

"So what you're saying is I'm a skillful kisser?"

"Maybe," she admitted.

"Maybe I'd have to say you ain't so bad yourself, lady."

He pointed skyward. Mistletoe still graced the archway, and the small pecks she'd offered no longer seemed adequate, not adequate at all. There was no longer any lingering awkwardness when they kissed, just an increasing sense of familiarity.

Libby welcomed the feel of his lips pressing against hers, welcomed the invigorating feeling of truly living that swept through her whenever they kissed. Fully alive—that's how Josh made her feel. Like she'd wasted years sleeping her life away, like some new-millennium Sleeping Beauty. Only, she'd never truly felt beautiful until Josh held her, until Josh kissed her.

She could stay like this forever.

"I love you, you know," he whispered.

Abruptly all her pleasant thoughts and feelings evaporated. Libby pushed free of his embrace. "No," she whispered.

Kissing him? She finally felt at home with that. But loving him?

"No," she said louder.

"Libby" was all he said, one word laced with pain.

But Libby couldn't deal with his pain, only her own. She repeated, "Don't say it."

He pulled her back into his embrace—a place she'd almost learned to feel at home during the last few weeks. But now there was no comfort in his arms, only the feeling that she had to get away. "No."

Josh dropped his arms, and let her put distance between them. Softly he said, "I know I haven't said the words before but surely you've realized where all these feelings were leading? I love you."

"You don't, though." He was on the rebound, or maybe he was lonely, moving back home to a city that had changed so much. Maybe it was just lust, or maybe it was the time of the year affecting his good sense, but whatever it was, Libby was sure that it wasn't love.

"I didn't want to love you, but I can't escape the feeling, Libby. It's palpable and it's growing. There was something there that first time we met."

"The only thing then was your truck blocking in my car. And the only thing here now is an old-fashioned case of lust. We've both been on our own for too long."

Trying to make him understand, she continued. "Maybe you think you love me now, but it won't last—it never does. What we were finding, well, it was enough. Being friends, and a little bit of lust, it was more than I expected. But I can't give you more than that—there's no more in my heart to offer, nothing left to give. It's too hard to try and believe anymore."

He glared at her. "Are you finished?"

"I was finished as soon as we began."

She ran from the room, stumbling in the doorway but catching herself. "I have to go now."

"Running, Libby? I thought you were a fighter," he taunted. "You've never had problems fighting me before. This once, instead of fighting me, couldn't you fight *for* me?"

She whirled on him. "I'm a fighter? Well, you were wrong. Sometimes it's better to run than stay and open yourself up for another wound."

Josh looked like he had more to say, but he didn't. He simply followed her. "I'll drive you home."

"I don't need you to do me any favors," she said. She worked the buttons on her coat with shaky hands.

"That's right, Libby McGuiness doesn't need any favors. She doesn't need anybody, does she?"

Her heart constricted as she said, "You're wrong about that, too." She needed Meg. Thinking of her daughter, the pain in Libby's chest eased. She had Meg and Meg had her. It had always been enough, and would be enough again when Josh was gone. "You're so wrong."

She tried to move past Josh, but his hand reached out and gripped her shoulder. "I said I'd drive you."

"Fine." She shrugged, dislodging his hand. "It'll save me from calling a cab."

She followed him to the truck, neither of them saying a word. The time for words was done, destroyed when Josh had uttered those three words to her, words he didn't mean, despite what he thought.

The drive was much longer than the couple miles Libby knew it to be. Josh's anger radiated like a brilliant red aura, filling the car like a physical presence.

It was easier that he was angry, easier than dealing with him being hurt. Hurting Josh was the last thing she wanted to do. She cared about him, though she knew he wouldn't believe that right now. She cared about him enough to keep him from saying things he'd come to realize he didn't mean.

He was on the rebound. They had a few things in common, like coffee and old movies. Add to that a smattering of lust, and it was easy to see how Josh might mistake what he felt as love.

But it wasn't.

Relief flooded her body as his truck pulled into her driveway. "Thank you," she whispered, pulling the handle of the door.

Once again, Josh's hand reached out and held her back. "What will it take to convince you that I love you?" he asked, his normally strong voice breaking.

"It's no use," she said, sad that it was true. "You're just reestablishing yourself and starting over. I think you haven't had time to really work out how you feel."

When Josh didn't respond, she rattled on. "It was enough of a risk dating you, but if you think you love me...? I can't do that to you. I can't do that to me. I can't do it to Meg."

"Don't use Meg as an excuse. She's fearless, she's wonderful…she's not an excuse."

"I'm not using her," Libby protested even as he pulled her closer, farther away from the door, his lips silencing her protests.

Hard and demanding, he kissed as if he was trying to imprint himself on her very soul.

"You can't get away from what's happening between us by running," he said as he pulled away. "There's something here, something that shouldn't be allowed to slip away. I wasn't looking for love any more than you were, but it's here between us, an undeniable force. Stop using your head, Libby. Use your heart instead."

His voice dropped to barely a whisper. "Because no matter what you say, your heart knows there's something significant going on here. It has nothing to do with me being on the rebound or being lonely. And your running away has nothing to do with Meg. You're so afraid because you know I'm right—the something between us is love, Libby. And these feelings aren't going to go away, they're not going to fade, no matter how far or how fast you run."

"Goodbye," she said as she pulled away from his embrace and bolted from the truck. She ran to the front door, pulling her keys from her heavy winter coat, fumbling as she tried to insert the right one into the lock.

"I'm sorry," she whispered as she opened the door and then firmly shut it when she was safe inside.

Her cheery Christmas decorations seemed to mock her as she walked through her living room to the kitchen. A kitchen where she'd spent so much time with Josh, laughing, touching…kissing. She stood in the middle of the room without bothering to remove her coat. She stared at the Christmas greens that draped the fireplace's mantle, but didn't really see them.

Love?

No, what he was feeling wasn't love. Lust and loneliness maybe, but not love.

And what she felt—what would she call that? Lust? Remembering how she'd felt in Josh's arms, her lips pressed to his, lust was certainly an apt description. And loneliness? As much as she loved Meg, she did miss a quiet companionship with a man, something she'd found in Josh. Right after they'd met, she'd said she wanted them to be friends. Well, she'd gotten that wish, and now she was going to lose that friendship.

If she had any tears left, she'd cry. But she'd used up all her tears years ago. They'd dried up along with her dreams of ever having a happily-ever-after.

But though she didn't believe in love, she did have feelings for Josh. Until now, when she'd lost him, she hadn't realized how much he'd come to mean to her.

Lost.

That was exactly the right word to describe how

Libby was feeling as she stood dry-eyed in the middle of her kitchen.

Josh drove home, wishing the roads were clear so that he could go fast. Not that speed would alleviate the pounding in his head and the aching of his heart.

He loved her.

Joshua Gardner loved Libby McGuiness—prickly, scared and running-as-fast-as-she-could Libby McGuiness.

She might deny his feelings and deny she had any feelings of her own, but he didn't believe it. She felt the rightness of their being together. She was just scared.

Well, dammit, so was he.

He'd given her five days' grace once before, and this one last time he'd give her some time and distance, and allow her to adjust to her new reality, a reality that included Josh loving her. But he wasn't giving up on her, wasn't giving up on them.

He and Lynn had given up on their marriage; neither of them had invested half the time and energy into keeping it alive. But Josh had learned from the past. What he felt for Libby was big, and it was worth fighting for. When he told her that there was something significant going on between them, it had been an understatement. They were meant for each other, whether Libby wanted to admit it or not.

So, yes, he'd give her some space to adjust, and

then he was going after her, going after what they could have.

When he'd first met Libby, she had seemed confident and independent; now she seemed lost and afraid. But Josh had found her, had found where they both belonged—they belonged with each other.

And Josh wasn't about to lose that.

Chapter Ten

"Mama," Meg said, fingers flying, hands dancing in her excitement. "There's a big car in the driveway." As if on cue, the doorbell rang and the light flashed in time to the ringer.

"Hold your pants on," Libby called as she hurried to the door, wiping her hands on a dish towel. "Can I help you?" she asked as she opened the door.

She immediately tried to slam it back in place, but it didn't budge.

"Don't," Josh told her.

"We ended this the other night." Five days. She'd left him five days ago, and when he didn't call, didn't stop by, Libby had assumed that it was over.

She should have known better. Josh had proven in the past that he was good at waiting.

"There was no 'we' about it. *You* ended our relationship and I didn't fight, but if you remember correctly, I didn't agree, either."

"Hey, sweetums," Pearly called, stepping out from behind Josh.

"What's going on?" Libby looked past Josh and directed her question to Pearly. Maybe if she ignored Josh, he'd go away.

"Why, Josh is taking you out for your night on the town. Remember?" She pointed to the driveway. "See? Your carriage awaits."

A huge stretch limo sat in the driveway.

Still blocking the door, Libby shook her head. "I'm not going."

"Why, of course you're going," Pearly said. She pushed past Josh and breezed right by Libby. "I'm here, so you don't have any excuse."

Pearly took off her coat and hung it on a hook. As if suddenly becoming aware of the silence in the small hall, she paused a moment and added, "Unless you're afraid to go for some reason?"

"I'm not afraid of anything." No, Libby wasn't afraid. She wasn't running no matter what anyone said. She'd made a decision based on what was best for her and for Meg.

In her primmest voice, she added, "Josh and I decided that there's nothing between us, is all. I don't see why we should go to dinner together."

"If there's nothing between us, there's no reason

not to go to dinner. Is there?'' Josh asked, obviously no longer content to let Pearly argue his case.

"Oh, go,'' Pearly said, waving aside Libby's arguments. "If you've decided that your relationship ended with the Christmas party, then this will give you what those fancy doctor books call *closure*. My mama would simply call it a free meal. And only a fool would pass up a free meal.''

She took Libby's coat off a hook and thrust it at her. "Meggie and I are going to make some Christmas cookies.''

Despite the fact her casual slacks weren't what she'd have chosen to wear for a night on the town, Libby found herself hustled into the back of the limo. They rode in silence for about five minutes. Libby barely glanced at the rich leather interior of the vehicle. She simply stared out the window, not really seeing downtown Erie pass by.

Finally, when the silence became so oppressive she could barely breathe, she whirled around and faced Josh. "We decided the other night we were over.''

"No, you decided, and you ran. I just let you, but I never said I wouldn't follow you.'' He pulled off his gloves and laid them between them on the seat.

"I'm getting sick of everyone playing armchair psychiatrist. You, Pearly, Josie, Mabel... You all keep harping about me running away. Pearly even used the term *closure!* Why is it everyone is analyzing me? What about you? You've mentioned an ex-wife, mentioned wanting kids. Maybe what you think you're feeling isn't real? Maybe you're just using me and Meg to fulfill some fantasy family you put together?''

"There would be easier ways to go about getting a family, if that was the only reason I wanted you. Let's face it, Libby. You're work." He paused and added, "Hard work."

"So why won't you give up?" *Give up,* she wanted to plead with him. She wasn't sure what to do with this man who wouldn't leave her alone. Why didn't he just walk away? Other people had no trouble walking out of her life. Mitch had left without a backward glance.

"You want to turn the tables and analyze me?" he asked. Josh had certainly spent enough time trying to figure himself out, and if Libby wanted to know, then he'd tell her.

"You're right. I wanted kids and Lynn didn't. But that's not why our marriage fell apart. I spent months wondering what happened between us, especially after I met you. I needed to understand what went wrong between Lynn and I because I didn't want to repeat the past."

"What did you decide?" she asked almost grudgingly.

Josh remembered his confusion when things had ended with Lynn. Confusion more than pain. They'd had a business partnership, but they hadn't really had a partnership in any way that really mattered.

"Somewhere along the line Lynn and I stopped noticing each other," he said. "We stopped working on our relationship. We had a business together and we both worked at that, but our marriage? We just let things slip until there wasn't enough feeling left to even work up to hating her when I found out she was cheating. I was furious and hurt when she filed for divorce, but much as I hated to admit it, there was almost a sense of relief."

"That doesn't explain why you won't let this go between us. I'm obviously no better at relationships than your ex-wife was."

"I'm not giving up on another relationship just because it's going to take a little work." He studied Libby a moment, a small grin on his face. "Okay, a lot of work."

"We don't have a relationship to work on."

He longed to reach across the small space that separated them and touch her, but he realized there was a bigger emotional separation he had to breach first. "I think we do have something worth working on. Our relationship is special."

"We don't have a relationship," she argued.

"We do. And it wasn't the idea of a relationship that sent you running. It took a while, but you'd adjusted to the idea of having a relationship with me. It was the idea of love that sent you running. And, Libby, there's nothing you can do to make me stop loving you. You can run, but I'll simply run right after you. I know you don't want to hear it, but there it is. I love you."

The window between the driver and the back seat slid down. "We're here," the man said. Then the window closed again.

"I'm not asking you to marry me, just have dinner with me."

"We don't have a relationship," Libby maintained. "We've gone on our limo ride. I agreed because we needed to talk, to put this behind us. We've talked, had our *closure*. There's nothing left to say. I'm ready to go home."

"You're running."

"No. I'm going home to my daughter and my life. There's a difference." She tapped the window, which lowered. "Just take me back, please."

Josh waited until the window was back in place before he said, "You're using Meg as an excuse. She deserves more than that from you. Like I said before, she's not an excuse."

Libby didn't dignify his statement with a retort. He was wrong. She was simply a realist. Whatever Josh's reasons for thinking he loved her, whatever fantasy he'd built up in his head, she knew better. A relationship between them would never work, and it was better to end things now before anyone got hurt.

She went back to staring out the window. It was easier than looking at Josh and seeing what appeared to be pain in his eyes. She didn't want to hurt him, but she would rather break things off now than hurt him more later.

Oh, hell, who was she kidding? Breaking things off to avoid hurting Josh sounded so noble, but she was honest enough with herself to admit that she was trying to save herself from being hurt.

They pulled into her driveway and Libby felt a rush of relief. It was over.

"Goodbye," she said. She opened the door and slammed it behind her; unfortunately it didn't shut.

"Can I come in?" Josh asked, the limo backing out of the driveway. "I sent the driver home, so I'm sort of stranded."

"Too bad." Libby knew she was being rude, but she didn't care. She didn't want Josh here. She didn't want the ache in her chest to start again. She didn't want to dream it could be different. And she most definitely didn't want to start to believe him when he said he loved her. If she did, her heart wouldn't just ache, but would shatter when he eventually left.

"We had our limo ride and our talk. You've had your say. Now it's time for you to go."

He pushed past her into her entryway and shut the door behind him. He stood there—filling her house with one more unwanted Joshua Gardner memory—studying her.

"What do I have to do to convince you it's over?" she cried.

"It'll never be over," Josh maintained softly.

"Josh…" Libby was interrupted by a thump behind her. Meg had stomped her foot to get her mother's attention. She was covered with flour and traces of the green cookie frosting lined her lips.

"Mom. You're home," she signed. "Pearly and I were baking. Do you want to help?" Meg glanced at Josh and smiled, nodding her head in greeting and giving him a little wave. "Josh can help, too."

"Slow," Josh signed to Meg. "I know *baking* and I know *help*. Me?" he asked, the question in his eyes.

Both Libby and Meg stared at him. Meg's fingers flew in his direction, but he just shrugged hopelessly, signing "Slow."

"You signed," Libby accused.

"I've been taking lessons."

"Lessons?" she asked.

"Yeah, you know, American Sign Language lessons. The teacher at the Mercyhurst party has been giving me private lessons so I could learn faster and tailor my learning to my needs. I've only had three classes, but I've been working at it. I can sign…" Slowly he signed, "My name is Joshua Gardner." He smiled as his fingers stumbled over a few of the letters.

"And I recognized *baking* and *help* in the middle of Meg's flying fingers." Meg was beaming and Libby just stood there, something big spreading through her chest, replacing the ache, replacing the fear.

Josh wasn't going to leave her house because she told him to, and suddenly Libby realized he wasn't going to leave her life, either. She could fight him, she could run.... Hell, all her armchair psychiatrists were right. Running—that's what she'd been doing since the very beginning, and yet, here he was, signing to her daughter.

When things got tough, Josh got tougher.

Since Mitch left, she'd been afraid to lean on anyone, afraid that when she needed them most they'd let her fall. As Mitch had. But Josh? She looked at him signing to Meg. Would that toughness be enough? Libby had a feeling that loving her could be very hard work—was Josh up to it? If she leaned, would he support her? And did she have the strength to support him in turn?

He stood there, chatting in terribly slow broken sign language to Meg, and the feeling that was spreading through her chest totally squeezed out the pain and fear. The feeling she'd been so afraid to name, so afraid to claim was bigger than even she could contain.

The feeling she'd never named was—

"Oh," Josh added, "I did learn a couple other phrases. Like..." And he signed, "Merry Christmas. I love Meg, I love Libby."

Tears she hadn't shed since that day so long ago when the doctor had told her Meg was deaf now stung her eyes. But this time there was no despair behind them.

"I love you, too," Meg signed with the freeness of a heart that had never been broken.

"Meg, leave your mom and Josh alone and come take care of your cookies," Pearly called, and Libby signed.

Meg rushed from the room, leaving Libby alone with Josh and the huge feeling that was rapidly becoming too big to contain.

She wanted to tell him, wanted to explain, but the words were lost; the signs were, as well. She stood mute with the growing realization that this man wouldn't leave, that no matter how she pushed, or what obstacles life threw at them, he wasn't going anywhere.

"There's one more thing I learned to say," Josh said, moving closer to Libby. Slowly his hands formed the words, "Will you marry me?"

The something that had been spreading through her chest suddenly broke free. With tears streaming down her face, she walked forward into Josh's open arms.

"You love me? You really love me," she half asked and half said.

"I love you," he whispered into her ear. "You can't shake me. You can be mean. You can kick me out. You can deny your feelings and walk away. But I'll still be here, still loving you and Meg. I'm in this for the long haul, no matter how much time, how much work it takes."

"You love us both?" She needed to be sure she heard him right, needed to hear him say the words, sign the words, again and again.

"Both. I want you both. I want us all to be a family. I love you, Libby. Nothing's going to change that. Marry me?"

She kissed him.

"Ah, we have company," he said, breaking the kiss off reluctantly.

Libby turned and looked at Meg and Pearly standing in the kitchen doorway, smiling broadly. "He wants to marry me," she signed.

"About time," Meg said.

"You can say that again," Pearly added. "I was beginning to worry that you were going to screw things up and then you'd regret it for—"

"Twenty-eight years, three months and four days," Libby supplied.

"I marry your mom?" Josh signed to Meg, totally ignoring Pearly and Libby's banter.

Meg just nodded enthusiastically. "Later. Now cookies, tomorrow Christmas, presents. Later marry." Her signs were slow and choppy as she tried to make her words easier for Josh to understand.

Meg turned to her mother. "Just tell Josh yes."

"You're sure?" Libby asked, though she hardly needed to. Meg's shining eyes gave her answer better than any words or signs could.

"Would you stop leaving the boy standing there waiting for your answer and just tell him yes," Pearly grumbled, and led Meg back into the kitchen.

"She says you can marry me later. Right now we

have baking and then tomorrow we have presents to open.''

Nervously he asked, ''She doesn't seem to mind?''

''Mind? No, she doesn't mind. She knows she's getting a built-in math tutor and video buddy.''

Libby kissed him again.

Josh dug through his pocket. ''Is that a yes?''

''Yes.'' Libby said the word and waited for an old stab of fear, but there was nothing but a feeling of rightness, a feeling of coming home.

''Here,'' he said, handing her a small gray box. ''I've been holding on to this for a while now.''

Libby opened the small box and gasped. Inside was a beautifully cut emerald ring. ''Josh, are you sure? I mean, taking on Meg and her problems and...''

Josh gently pushed the ring over her knuckle, then he kissed her. ''Meg's the least of my worries. I figure between the classes and the practice I get here, I'll be signing soon. And communication was Meg's and my biggest hurdle. She's a loving and trusting girl. She's not a deaf girl, she's a girl who just can't hear. No, my problems have never been Meg. It's been her wildly stubborn, hardheaded mother.''

''Well, for the record, her wildly stubborn hardheaded mother seems to have fallen in love with you, too,'' Libby confessed.

''I know,'' Josh told her smugly.

''You know? Is that all you have to say?''

Josh didn't say anything, but his fingers moved slowly, signing, "I love you, too."

The moment was broken as they both turned to the stomping coming from the kitchen door. "Are you two going to kiss all day? We have cookies to finish and then we have to make the fudge."

"I caught *cookies*," Josh said, laughing.

Libby's laughter joined his. "Seems after the cookies, we have to make the fudge."

"I love you," he whispered as they followed Meg into the kitchen.

"I love you, too," Libby signed.

She stood in the doorway, watching him frost cookies with Pearly and Meg. The something growing in her chest was overwhelming. It was something big, something significant.... It most definitely was love.

* * * * *

Look for

READY, WILLING...AND ABEL?
and RAISING CAIN,

two linked stories in one compelling volume,
only from Holly Jacobs and Harlequin Duets.

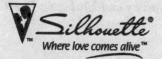

If you enjoyed what you just read,
then we've got an offer you can't resist!

Take 2 bestselling
love stories FREE!

Plus get a FREE surprise gift!

Clip this page and mail it to Silhouette Reader Service™

IN U.S.A.
3010 Walden Ave.
P.O. Box 1867
Buffalo, N.Y. 14240-1867

IN CANADA
P.O. Box 609
Fort Erie, Ontario
L2A 5X3

YES! Please send me 2 free Silhouette Romance® novels and my free surprise gift. After receiving them, if I don't wish to receive anymore, I can return the shipping statement marked cancel. If I don't cancel, I will receive 6 brand-new novels every month, before they're available in stores! In the U.S.A., bill me at the bargain price of $3.15 plus 25¢ shipping and handling per book and applicable sales tax, if any*. In Canada, bill me at the bargain price of $3.50 plus 25¢ shipping and handling per book and applicable taxes**. That's the complete price and a savings of at least 10% off the cover prices—what a great deal! I understand that accepting the 2 free books and gift places me under no obligation ever to buy any books. I can always return a shipment and cancel at any time. Even if I never buy another book from Silhouette, the 2 free books and gift are mine to keep forever.

215 SEN DFNQ
315 SEN DFNR

Name	(PLEASE PRINT)	
Address	Apt.#	
City	State/Prov.	Zip/Postal Code

* Terms and prices subject to change without notice. Sales tax applicable in N.Y.
** Canadian residents will be charged applicable provincial taxes and GST.
   All orders subject to approval. Offer limited to one per household and not valid to
   current Silhouette Romance® subscribers.
   ® are registered trademarks of Harlequin Enterprises Limited.